NEW BEGINNINGS—
NOT MY WILL

BOOK ONE

Stephanie Fleming
Shelly Funk

New Harbor Press

RAPID CITY, SD

Copyright © 2024 by Stephanie Fleming and Shelly Funk

All rights reserved. No part of this publiation may be reproduced, distributed or transmitted in any form or by any means, without prior written permission.

Funk & Fleming/New Harbor Press
1601 Mt.Rushmore Rd, Ste 3288
Rapid City, SD 57701
www.newharborpress.com

New Beginnings—Not My Will/Stephanie Fleming and Shelly Funk. -- 1st ed.
ISBN 978-1-63357-454-0

CONTENTS

CHAPTER ONE 1
CHAPTER TWO 7
CHAPTER THREE 13
CHAPTER FOUR 19
CHAPTER FIVE 25
CHAPTER SIX 31
CHAPTER SEVEN 39
CHAPTER EIGHT 47
CHAPTER NINE 53
CHAPTER TEN 59
CHAPTER ELEVEN 69
CHAPTER TWELVE 79
CHAPTER THIRTEEN 89
CHAPTER FOURTEEN 97
CHAPTER FIFTEEN 105
CHAPTER SIXTEEN 109
CHAPTER SEVENTEEN 117
CHAPTER EIGHTEEN 123
CHAPTER NINETEEN 129
CHAPTER TWENTY 135
CHAPTER TWENTY-ONE 141
CHAPTER TWENTY-TWO 147
CHAPTER TWENTY-THREE 153
CHAPTER TWENTY-FOUR 161

CHAPTER TWENTY-FIVE 167
CHAPTER TWENTY-SIX 173
CHAPTER TWENTY-SEVEN 179
CHAPTER TWENTY-EIGHT 185
CHAPTER TWENTY-NINE 191
CHAPTER THIRTY 197
CHAPTER THIRTY-ONE 203
CHAPTER THIRTY-TWO 209
CHAPTER THIRTY-THREE 217

CHAPTER ONE

Jexi stood on the back deck of the cruise ship alone and stared numbly into the enveloping black of the night. She shivered as she felt a cool breeze blow across her face. Her long black hair tickled her shoulders as the air moved it back and forth. The moon and the stars were clearly visible due to the cloudless sky and Jexi found herself enthralled with their exquisite beauty.

She yawned and then glanced at her watch. Twelve forty-five a.m. She should be asleep. As tired as she was though, she just could not bring herself to go to bed. Frankly, there were just too many things on her mind.

So much had happened over the past couple of days and Jexi just could not make sense of any of it. She allowed herself to revisit the recent events and she felt her eyes swell with tears. Yesterday was supposed to be her wedding day. The happiest day of her life, or so she thought. She placed her right hand on top of her left. She felt the empty groove on her ring finger where her wedding ring should have been sitting. As her tears landed on the empty indention, each moment of the agonizing day replayed in her mind.

It was going to be a perfect and magical day. Everyone and everything was exactly as she had been dreaming of since she was a little girl.

The ceremony had been planned to the minutest of details. She was getting married in her mom and dad's church. The pastor who had baptized her parents was going to be the one to join her with the man she loved. The sanctuary was decorated in a lovely and enchanting way. Purple roses and white calla lilies dyed with purple and teal were tied to the end of each pew with teal ribbons and lace. They were the exact match for the large bouquet she was to carry. Dozens of LED candles had been strategically placed throughout the sanctuary to provide a beautiful flickering effect. Small twinkle lights were stretched across the front of the room. She smiled as she remembered her mother taking picture after picture and gushing over her vision.

The reception was to be held in the all-purpose room in the back of the church. The entrance had a massive arch decorated with draping purple wisteria, baby's breath, and more twinkling lights. The room itself had purple-and-teal canopies wrapped in twinkling lights, cascading from each corner to a chandelier in the center. The wedding party table in the front of the room was also decorated with purple roses and calla lilies. The wisteria added an unexpected elegance, pouring over the front of the table and reaching the floor. Each guest table had been covered with purple or teal tablecloths. The centerpiece on each table consisted of three clear tubes filled with water and purple hibiscus flowers. Each tube had a tea light floating on the liquid. Jexi remembered feeling dreamily happy looking at it all. Her mother and her best friend, Shaya, had really outdone themselves.

The honeymoon had also been booked. They were taking a seven-day cruise to Aruba. Bags were packed and transportation to the airport in Miami had been arranged. All of the items had been checked off her list one by one. All that was left was the wedding itself.

Thinking back on it all, she recalled waking up so excitedly. She was going to marry the love of her life! She seemed to float through the day and through the various tasks. She and her bridesmaids slept as late as possible and spent the morning giggling and dressing to go to the salon. They made it to their first stop at ten o'clock in the morning for their pedicures and manicures. Her nails were done in a French manicure style with lavender tips. Simple, yet beautiful. Then she and the girls went across town for lunch. She had been too nervous to eat much but she knew she needed food to get through the day. After lunch, the wedding troupe made their way to the most prominent hair salon in town. This had been a gift from her dad. He was going to let her and her friends get their hair done by the famous local hairdresser, Jean Phillipe. Jexi decided to wear her hair down, with ringlet curls to frame her face. Brennan, her fiancé, always complimented her beauty when she wore her hair down.

Finally, everyone had gone to the church. With her mother's help, she stepped into her wedding gown. She felt like a princess wearing her dress. It was made of flowy chiffon and had a faux diamond bodice with cap sleeves. Her mother zipped up the back of her dress and Jexi turned around to face her. Her mother started to cry. Through her tears, her mother said, "Brennan will melt when he sees you!"

She felt giddy with anticipation. Then, it was time. The guests were seated and chatting quietly. Her dad was waiting anxiously to walk her down the aisle. The pianist was playing beautifully. There was only one thing wrong. Brennan wasn't there.

At first, she didn't panic. She even chuckled a bit to herself. It was just like Brennan to be late. He was late for just about everything, so she didn't bother getting angry. Who knows what could have happened? Maybe he had been hanging out with his buddies and lost track of time. But he would be there. He wouldn't miss this. She was sure of it. When they had seen each other last, two days ago, he was just as excited as she had been.

But soon it was almost seven o'clock and her guests were getting restless. And honestly, so was she. Being a few minutes late was not a big deal, but almost an hour? Something had to be wrong, she thought. Jexi had tried to call him several times but there was no answer. She paced back and forth, vaguely listening as her mother also made phone calls trying to find him. Her mother was calling friends, hospitals, and even police stations, but to no avail. Her dad and brother had gone to his apartment, but no one answered the door. They had gone out driving around trying to spot him. She texted her brother, "Anything?"

She whimpered when she read the response, "No, sorry."

Where could he be? she wondered. Is he hurt somewhere? Has there been an accident? The thought that he might have stood her up filled her mind with dread, but she immediately dismissed it. No, Brennan wouldn't have done that to her. There had to be a logical explanation. Her mom kept trying to come up with good reasons for his absence, but it did not help. Jexi had become frantically worried. Finally, at seven thirty-seven, her cell phone rang. It was Brennan. A huge wave of relief flooded through her. As she answered her phone, Jexi wanted to yell at him but maintained her composure.

"Where are you?" she demanded.

"I am at Charlie's Bar," he responded. She did not expect to hear him say that. Nor did she expect what she heard next. He spoke precisely as if he had been rehearsing. "Jexi, I thought I was in love with you and ready for marriage. But I'm not." Then silence. The relief that she had found suddenly changed to heartbreak. He wasn't coming.

Jexi felt her heart sink to the bottom of her feet and her mind swirled with confusion. She was speechless. What? He wasn't ready for marriage? Not in love with her? Where was this coming from? What about the past three years? Hadn't they meant anything to him? And how in the world am I supposed to be okay with this? We have been planning this wedding for months! How could he be saying these things?

She tried desperately to make words come out of her mouth, but she could not make a sound. A thousand thoughts and questions raced through her mind. But before she could utter a single word, Brennan broke the silence. "It's better this way," he said. "This way we save ourselves the pain of a divorce."

The silence resumed. Despite her best efforts, she still could not make herself produce a solitary sound. Did he wonder why she wasn't saying anything? She finally managed to croak out, "But what about—?" but he cut her off.

"I will get with you in a couple of weeks to handle things like returning the wedding gifts and stuff. Trust me, Jexi. It really is better this way." Then the line went dead. Did she just get dumped on her wedding day? In all her life, she never would have imagined this happening to her. She dropped the phone to the ground. If it hadn't been for Shaya's arm supporting her, Jexi would have fallen to the ground as well.

She looked up and saw her mom's eyes searching for answers. As soon as Jexi's tearful gaze met hers, a look of understanding crossed her mother's face and she immediately reached out and hugged her. She gingerly asked, "He's not coming?" Jexi could only shake her head no. "I'll call your father," her mother whispered, and walked quietly out of the bridal dressing room.

Jexi fell backward onto the couch. She was a tornado of emotions. She was trying to convince herself it was all a bad dream, but she could not ignore reality. Brennan did not want to marry her. She looked down at her dress, so lovingly picked out after trying on dozens of dresses. She gently felt the chiffon and lace as tears continued to stream down her face. She remembered how ecstatic she felt when she finally found THE dress. She had thought it was the perfect accent for such a wonderful relationship. What was she supposed to do now?

Shaya knelt in front of Jexi and took her hands. They sat silently like that for several minutes. Finally, Shaya spoke. "Let's get you home," she said.

Jexi looked up with tears spilling out of her eyes. She shakily queried, "What about the guests?"

Shaya softly replied, "Your parents are probably taking care of that right now. You don't need to worry about it."

"What am I supposed to do?" Jexi asked.

Shaya hugged her and said, "You take it one day at a time. And I'll be right by your side every step of the way. But first, let's go home."

Jexi barely remembered what happened after that. She vaguely recollected changing out of her wedding dress and into what should have been her honeymoon outfit. Shaya drove her home and stayed on the couch overnight. The last thing Jexi remembered was crying herself to sleep.

Jexi shook her head and brought herself back to the present moment. She didn't really want to be here, but it seemed terrible to allow the cruise tickets to go to waste. Besides, Brennan had told Shaya that he didn't want the ticket back and there was no way to get a refund, especially a day before the cruise. So, she and Shaya decided to go together. Shaya told her it would be a good way to get her mind off the wedding that didn't happen, but Jexi wasn't so sure about that. After all, this was supposed to be her honeymoon.

Jexi thought about her best friend sleeping in their shared cruise cabin. She was sure blessed to have someone so loyal in her life. Not only had Shaya spent the night at her apartment, but she had also handled the cruise details with Brennan so that Jexi wouldn't have to talk to him. And she took the time off work so that she could accompany Jexi on the cruise. She had stepped up and helped through the whole situation and Jexi was so very thankful.

She yawned again and decided that she needed to go to sleep. She wasn't sure how she was going to shut her brain down, but she hadn't slept much the night before and she was extremely exhausted. She walked back to the cabin and quietly opened the door with the key. She changed into her night clothes as quietly as possible and climbed into her cot. It was almost two a.m., and she knew that breakfast would come bright and early. She closed her eyes and allowed the gentle rocking of the waves soothe her to sleep. The last thing she remembered before dozing off was what Brennan had to say right before he hung up: "Trust me, Jexi. It really is better this way."

CHAPTER TWO

Jexi awoke to the sound of Shaya drying her hair. She rubbed her eyes and sat up. "Morning, sleepy head!" Shaya called over the din of the hairdryer. "You must have stayed out late last night!" Jexi tossed off the covers as Shaya turned off the blow-dryer.

"I couldn't sleep," Jexi replied. "I was still in too much shock, I guess." She watched Shaya massage a dab of hair gel into her curly auburn locks.

Shaya walked to her suitcase to select an outfit for the day. "Are you hungry?" she asked as she picked out her clothes. "I am going to change and then I will be ready for breakfast."

Jexi's stomach growled at the mention of food. Yes, she was hungry. She hadn't eaten much over the past two days. "Yes, I am very hungry," Jexi replied. "Let me get ready real quick."

Shaya laughed. "Real quick? Yeah, right!"

Jexi felt herself grin for the first time in two days. It actually felt kind of nice. "Okay, give me twenty minutes."

Forty minutes later, Shaya was still scrolling through her phone, bored. "Come on, already!" she yelled into the bathroom. Jexi stepped out and grabbed her purse. "Finally!" Shaya exclaimed.

Jexi giggled. "Well, I had to figure out what to wear. It's hard to make decisions when you're hungry and sleep-deprived."

Shaya picked up her purse and reached for the door handle. She opened the door and the two of them walked out of the cabin. "Got your key?" Shaya asked Jexi.

"Yup," Jexi replied. She patted her back pocket. "Right here."

They walked down to the breakfast buffet, lightheartedly teasing each other along the way. When they got to the buffet, Jexi was shocked to see the amount of food available. Food of every kind imaginable was spread from wall to wall. They had eggs prepared in every way known to man. There were hash browns, grits, French toast, bagels, pancakes, waffles, biscuits, and all kinds of flavored bread. There was a plethora of different cereals. Jexi's mouth watered and she wondered how much she could eat without getting sick.

There was a large variety of fruit and some that she had never even seen before. They had wraps, granola parfait, danishes, croissants, and muffins. They had bacon, sausage, ham, and breakfast steaks. They even had alcoholic beverages!

Shaya laughed and said, "I am going to gain twenty pounds this week! This food looks amazing!"

Jexi laughed in response and grabbed her stomach. "So much for dieting to fit into my wedding dress!"

Shaya rolled her eyes and reminded her, "We are NOT going to talk about that right now. We have a food coma to get to."

Jexi nodded and agreed. "Right. Priorities."

They both jumped into line. After they had filled their plates to the brim, they found a table near the window and sat down to eat. It was silent for a while as they both stared out at the sea while they munched.

Shaya broke the silence. "It's going to be okay, Jex. Trust God to heal your heart."

Jexi sighed and shook her head. "I just can't see how right now. I don't think my heart will ever heal."

They finished their breakfast and headed to the exit, both waddling and groaning from their full stomachs. Shaya looked at the ship's activities that were posted on the bulletin board in the main lobby. "What should we do today?"

Jexi wasn't really in the mood to do anything but sulk in the cabin, but she knew that Shaya would never let that happen. She also didn't want Brennan's decision to ruin this trip with her best friend. She was determined to survive this tragedy somehow and she figured this could be her first step. She would never forgive him for this but that didn't mean she couldn't have fun. What better revenge?

"There is a cooking demonstration in thirty minutes. What about that?" Shaya asked with minimal enthusiasm.

Jexi pointed into her open mouth in a show of gagging and replied, "I can't possibly look at food right now."

After glancing over all of the different activities, Jexi and Shaya filled their day with walking around an art gallery, playing bingo, shopping, playing table tennis, and taking a nap. It was easy to skip lunch since their breakfast had been so enormous. A small ice cream cone that afternoon seemed to satiate both of their appetites.

Dinner for both of them was light but filling and they talked about their plans for the evening. Jexi had heard that there was a comedian aboard and tried coaxing Shaya into going.

"Oh, please?" Jexi begged. "He is supposed to be hilarious, and I need to laugh. Let's go. Do it for me?"

"You know how much I hate to laugh!" exclaimed Shaya. And they both burst into uncontrollable giggles. The couple at the table next to them shot dirty looks their way. The two tried to quiet down but the more they tried, the louder they laughed.

"Let's go ahead and go now," said Shaya, "before this couple complains to management!" They ran out of the dining hall with people watching and some laughing along with them.

The comedian was a riot, just as Jexi had anticipated and they both laughed so hard they cried. As they walked out after the show, Jexi enjoyed the feeling of lightheartedness.

"Thanks, Shaya," she said with sadness in her voice. They both knew that she was talking about more than just going to the show.

"Shut up and quit being so mushy," Shaya said with a smile, which sent the two into more fits of laughter. They laughed all the way back to the cabin. It had been a memorable first day at sea.

The next morning, Jexi and Shaya arose late and headed to the breakfast buffet.

"Don't let me eat as much as I did yesterday," said Jexi.

Shaya laughed and said, "Who is going to stop me from doing the same thing?"

They decided during breakfast that they were just going to lie next to the pool and read that day. Yesterday was fun but tiring. They went to the cabin, changed into their swimsuits, and headed to the pool.

After a few hours, Shaya sat straight up and gasped.

Jexi woke up from her nap. "What?" she asked.

Shaya looked like she'd seen a ghost. "It can't be," she said. "That would not be possible!"

Jexi asked again, "What?"

Shaya shook her head. "I just saw someone who looked like someone I once knew, but it couldn't be. Never mind."

Jexi looked at Shaya and asked with annoyance, "Quit being so cryptic. Who was it? Tell me!"

"I had this boyfriend in high school who I thought I would someday marry. Unfortunately, we broke up after our first year of college. End of story. I saw someone who looked like him, only older," Shaya stated, with a hint of heartbreak.

"You never told me that!" Jexi exclaimed. "I need details. Now!" she demanded.

Shaya sighed, "Nothing to tell. It was young love. It didn't work out the way I expected, and it never occurred to me to mention it to you. It seems like so long ago. But I'm sure that wasn't him."

Jexi peppered Shaya with questions. "What was his name? Was he cute? Why would he let you go? How long were you together? Have you ever seen him again?"

Shaya rolled her eyes. "Wow, slow your roll! You are so nosy."

Jexi replied, "I'm your best friend. I have a right to know. Plus, we are here to take my mind off my troubles, aren't we? Spill!"

"Okay, okay!" Shaya said. "His name is Ben, Benjamin Thatcher. We started dating during our sophomore year of high school and stayed together through our first year of college."

"WHAT?" Jexi interrupted, "You didn't think a four-year relationship was worth sharing with your best friend?"

"I'm sorry, Jex. It just brings up a lot of old feelings and I don't like to talk about him," Shaya said. "After a year of a long-distance relationship, we just drifted apart. Honestly, we never really even broke up. We just stopped communicating. It's possible we are still dating." Shaya smiled sheepishly at her best friend, who was looking at her with wide eyes. "And yes . . . he was gorgeous!"

Jexi looked at her best friend. "Wow, Shay. I had no idea! That had to hurt. But, are you sure that the guy you saw just now wasn't him?"

Shaya shrugged, "What are the chances of an old high school boyfriend from Kansas would be on the same cruise ship to Aruba at the same exact time as us? I'm fairly certain it isn't Ben."

Jexi giggled, "Wouldn't that be wild? I lose my love and you find yours! We just have to find out if it's him or not! Which way did he go?"

"Go back to sleep, you crazy nut. I didn't even see where he went." Shaya responded.

"Fine,' Jexi mumbled. "I'll let it go. For now."

The girls gathered their belongings and went back to the cabin to shower and get ready for dinner. Jexi was still ruminating about Shaya possibly reconnecting with an old flame. But that would be an insane coincidence.

"I got it!" yelled Jexi from the bathroom as she was putting on her makeup. "Do an Internet search for his name!" She noticed Shaya was giving her a puzzled look. "Right now!" she added.

"What is wrong with you? I never said I wanted to find him." laughed Shaya.

Jexi jumped with excitement. "Maybe he is still in love with you too!" she yelled.

"Change of subject," Shaya said. "What are we doing after dinner? What is on the schedule for entertainment tonight?"

"We are going sleuthing," Jexi replied. "Just like Sherlock Holmes. I'll be your Watson!"

"Are we going to hunt for dead bodies?" Shaya asked sarcastically.

"No way, you weirdo!" Jexi answered. "We are going to hunt for a LIVE body! And his name is Ben!"

Shaya picked up the ship's entertainment guide and shook her head. "Sleuthing is not in the brochure, but there is a gospel hour in the Grand Duchess Room at eight o'clock. How does that sound?"

Jexi's mood deflated. "Really?" Jexi asked skeptically. "Gospel hour? I dunno," she hesitated.

"Come on! I listened to that hideous comedian for you last night. You can listen to some Jesus music for me," Shaya said.

"He wasn't hideous. He was hilarious. And you know it. But, yeah, I suppose you're right. I'll humor you this time," Jexi stated.

"Hideous, hilarious . . . whatever you want to call it," Shaya said through her laughter.

"Oh, alright," Jexi consented. "I'll go listen to your Jesus music. But I don't have to like it."

Shaya smiled. "You'll like it. I promise."

Jexi paused. "Shay, I know that you are convinced that God is with us always. But after last week, I'm just not sure. I can't imagine that God would have allowed this to happen or would want me to feel this kind of pain." She fought back a tear that threatened to fall. "But I'll go with you."

Shaya hugged her friend and whispered, "Maybe He has something better for you."

Jexi didn't respond but doubted her friend's wisdom. What could He possibly have that would be better than Brennan?

CHAPTER THREE

The two set off toward the Grand Duchess Room. It was on the opposite end of the ship and one level down, so they had a long walk.

As they reached the ship's grand staircase, Jexi squealed with delight. "Wow, this is the most beautiful surface my feet have ever touched!" She reached for the crystal handrails that enclosed a waterfall of steps that sparkled like diamonds in the sunshine. Jexi was entranced by the elegance that lay before her.

Shaya shrugged nonchalantly and stated, "It looks like someone spilled their canister of glitter!" Jexi gave Shaya an annoyed look, which made Shaya laugh and correct herself. "Okay, you win! This is AMAZING! I wonder if this is what Heaven will look like?"

It took a while to reach the bottom of the steps because the two of them took an abundance of photographs on the way down. Unfortunately, their phone cameras could not capture the breathtaking beauty they were experiencing.

"Look, Shaya," said Jexi, "I'm on the Titanic!" Jexi swayed gracefully down the staircase and pretended to give a queen's wave.

"Yeah, you are! After the show, we'll head out to the front of the ship and pretend to fly in the wind, just like in the movie. Just don't fall in the water because I won't be able to save you," Shaya quipped.

"Oh, ha ha!" Jexi replied sarcastically. "Let's just hope that this ship doesn't sink!"

"We need to hurry," Shaya announced. "The show starts in ten minutes!" They took one final photo and rushed to the Grand Duchess Room. The lights were already dim, so they had to peer around the room to find two open seats together. Jexi quickly pointed to two seats about halfway back in the center section and the girls rushed over to sit down. Once they were seated, Shaya leaned over and whispered, "What a great view!"

Jexi silently nodded in agreement. She did not want to admit it to Shaya, but she was slightly uncomfortable. She wasn't really sure of what to expect from this show. She had been contemplating her religious beliefs a lot lately. Would the people around her sense how she was feeling about God? She was not raised in church, but she knew a little about God. Her parents started attending church later in life. Jexi never really wanted to go with them. She had been a few times, but she hadn't been to church in a very long time, nor had she prayed in a very long time either. She desperately wanted the things she thought about God to be true. But with everything that happened, especially with the wedding, she was beginning to doubt that a loving God would allow her to suffer like this. She wondered where He was and why He hadn't stopped that tragedy from materializing. As she sat waiting for the show to start, she permitted herself a moment of honesty. She was extremely hurt, yes, but she was also very angry. Angry at Brennan and angry at God. If there really is a God, she thought to herself.

As Jexi was lost in her thoughts and wrestling with her beliefs, she did not notice a young man walk out onto the stage, bring out some equipment, adjust a few things on stage, and return to the back. Jexi heard Shaya gasp and she was jolted back to the moment.

Shaya whispered, "There's just no way . . ." and her voice trailed off. Her face was ashen, and her mouth gaped open.

Jexi turned toward her friend. "What is it?" she asked.

"It just . . . it just can't be," stuttered Shaya. "The odds of him being here . . . it just can't be!"

Jexi was happy for the distraction and her face lit up with a smile. "Ben?" she inquired. "Did you see him? Where?"

Shaya looked confused and hopeful at the same time. "The guy on the stage just now . . . did you see him?"

Jexi shook her head, "No, sorry. I was sort of . . . lost in thought."

"I need to get another look at that guy. Where did he go? He looks just like Ben, only older. But surely Ben wouldn't be on this cruise ship. Right?" Shaya's voice had gone up an octave and she was starting to sweat.

"Maybe he went backstage," Jexi pondered and thought about the situation. "Wait, I've got an idea!" she exclaimed excitedly. "What we do is wait until after the show for everyone to leave. Then we block the only entrance, and you will run into him for sure!"

"NO WAY! I don't really want to run into him, I just want to get a look at him. Because what if it really IS Ben? What would I even say to him? 'Umm, "Hi Ben, how are you? And by the way, are we still dating?"'" Shaya said with panic in her voice.

Jexi giggled. "Okay, so maybe not that, but you could make small talk. You know how to do that!"

The band began walking onto the stage and the crowd grew quiet and began to applaud. There was an excited anticipation in the air and Shaya was a bundle of nerves. She seemed relieved that the band had come out and they could quickly end the conversation.

But something inside Jexi told her that the mystery guy really was Ben and that, somehow, the two would reconnect. She really wanted to make that happen for Shaya. But how?

The band started to play an upbeat song. Jexi had never heard it before, but she liked the music. She even found herself tapping her feet to the beat. The lyrics to the songs were displayed on the screens on either side of the room.

The audience was singing along with the band and everyone gave the impression that they were so happy. As Jexi looked around at the people near her, they appeared to be lost in the music as they praised the Lord. Several had their hands raised, some seemed to be in prayer, and some of them were crying. That's new, thought Jexi. She had never seen anyone cry while singing in church. She glanced over at Shaya, who had her eyes closed. She wasn't singing. She was simply standing with her arms raised. Jexi wondered what she was doing. She really didn't know what to make of all this. The music at her parents' church was nothing like this when she had attended.

Jexi turned her attention to the words of the songs. The lyrics of each song talked about a God who loves her and will protect and shelter her. She was skeptical and was attempting to reconcile that God with the God that she felt was punishing her. Deep down, she felt a stir, but she was not completely sure what it was. Where was God's protection and shelter when Brennan abandoned her? She began to feel tears sting her eyes. She felt the heat of anger rise up her neck and her heart felt heavy. She leaned over to Shaya and whispered, "I need to get out of here." Before Shaya could respond, Jexi grabbed her purse, quickly stepped into the aisle, and left the room.

Shaya gathered her things and took off after her. When Shaya reached the lobby, she saw Jexi running up the stairs. "Jex, wait for me!" she called, as she bounded after her to close the distance.

Jexi stopped running at the top of the stairs and turned around. Her face was streaked with tears and her chest was heaving with heavy breaths.

Shaya didn't ask what was wrong. She didn't have to. She simply opened her arms to Jexi and allowed Jexi to fall into her embrace and cry on her shoulder. The two stood this way for a few minutes. Neither girl was even conscious of anyone else around them. Jexi had been holding these tears back for several days, but it now felt nice to be able to release it all.

"Why?" Jexi whimpered to Shaya between sobs. "Why? Why me? What did I do to deserve this?"

Shaya pushed Jexi back and grabbed her by the shoulders. "Jex, listen! You did NOTHING to deserve this! Brennan is a jerk! You were the best thing to ever happen to him, and he's an idiot to let you go." Shaya took a breath and continued. "This is not your fault. You have experienced a tragedy and it's okay to feel this badly. But you also have to accept the fact that it did happen. The good news is that it is over now and, eventually, you will be okay. You may not want to hear this right now, but God will help you through it if you let Him."

Jexi looked down at the ground. She retrieved a tissue from her purse and blew her nose. She remained silent for several seconds. She then looked up at Shaya and said, "I'd like to go back to the cabin. You don't have to come with me, but I am really tired, and I want to lie down."

Shaya moved next to Jexi and put her arm over her shoulder. "I'm not leaving you alone. You're stuck with me."

The girls walked in silence back to their cabin. Jexi was relieved to have Shaya by her side, and she was able to calm down while they walked.

When they returned to the cabin, Jexi crawled into her cot while Shaya went to the bathroom to remove her makeup. Jexi grabbed the romance novel she had been reading at the time. She scoffed as she looked at the picture on the cover. The couple pictured looked so happy as they embraced each other. Jexi rolled her eyes. That doesn't happen in real life, she thought. Then she scowled as another thought crossed her mind. Is true love even a real thing or do people just tolerate each other? she pondered.

She put the book back on the nightstand. She didn't feel like reading it. She wished she had a murder mystery novel instead. She could pretend that Brennan was the victim, and his body was buried in her mom's flower bed.

Jexi stood up and headed toward the bathroom for her turn at removing her makeup and brushing her teeth. While she was scrubbing her face she peeked out of the bathroom at Shaya.

"Hey, Shaya," she inquired, "If God is so good, how come He is doing this to me?"

Shaya turned to Jexi and gently said, "He is not 'doing' anything to you. We live in a fallen world, and we all have free will. Brennan used his free will to hurt you deeply. But God loves you so much and He wants to heal your heart. I promise that if you turn to Him, you will experience a peace that you can't explain. Hold on, let me read you something." Jexi watched as Shaya dug through her suitcase and pulled out a leather Bible. She thumbed through the pages. "Here it is. It's Philippians four, verses six and seven. 'Do not be anxious about anything, but in everything by prayer and supplication with thanksgiving let your requests be made known to God. And the peace of God, which surpasses all understanding will guard your hearts and your minds in Christ Jesus.'"

Jexi looked at her with bewilderment. "In layman's terms, please? What does that mean?"

Shaya giggled. "It means that we don't need to worry about anything because we have the peace of God. And when we have His peace, we can remain calm despite what is happening in the world."

"I still don't get it. How can God's peace keep you calm when everything is chaos around you?" Jexi asked.

"It's hard to explain," Shaya replied. "It is more of a sense of knowing that no matter what happens, God is going to hold us close and carry us through the hard times."

Jexi nodded. She was slowly beginning to understand what Shaya was saying, but she still couldn't completely see how God could calm her despondent heart. She also couldn't comprehend how God was not doing this to her. Doesn't God control everything? If He does, then why would he let Brennan leave her heartbroken?

"Thanks, Shaya," Jexi said. "But that is a lot to take in. My head is spinning!"

Shaya grinned. "I understand. Let's get to bed. We dock in Aruba tomorrow and we want to be nice and refreshed for the beach!"

Jexi turned off the lights and they both climbed into their beds. The darkness enveloped Jexi and she allowed it to carry her off to sleep.

CHAPTER FOUR

The next morning the girls awoke at seven o'clock to the sound of Shaya's alarm. The pair was excited to get to the beach in Aruba and were looking forward to doing some shopping. They dressed and packed up everything they thought they would need for the day, including that ridiculous romance novel for a little beach reading. They then rushed to the dining room and quickly ate breakfast at the buffet.

After breakfast, they hurried to the ramp on the boat that took them to the dock. When they stepped off the dock onto the island, the girls looked around in awe. The beauty and busyness of the island were breathtaking. They began walking down the main street where they saw shops of every kind. The main strip was full of people going in every which way. Shop owners were haggling with tourists or calling out to tourists to convince them to stop at their stores. Jexi couldn't help but think how much she would have loved being here with Brennan. He had gone out of his way to make this a perfect honeymoon. But she had to remember that she was not here with him. The mere thought made her heart ache, but she was determined to make the best of a nasty situation. At least she could focus on having a fabulous time with Shaya.

The girls had a full morning of shopping, giggling, and trying on silly hats and other accessories. They bought several souvenirs and some authentic Aruba aloe. They took a lot of pictures and made a plethora of memories. They were surprised when Shaya looked at her watch and announced that it was almost noon! The morning had flown by very quickly.

Jexi's stomach growled. "I'm starved!" she exclaimed. "Let's find some lunch!"

"Yes, please! You are reading my mind." Shaya responded.

Jexi took out the tourist map of restaurants in the area and scanned it. "How are we going to decide where to eat? Should we ask a local?"

Shaya took the map of restaurants from Jexi. "Nope," she said. She closed her eyes, pointed her finger above the map, and began to move her hand around in a circular motion. With her eyes still closed, she brought her finger down onto the map. "We will eat here," she stated and then opened her eyes. "It's called The Paddock."

Jexi smiled. "I love how scientifically you made your selection!" she said sarcastically.

"Well, I'm starving, and we don't have time for chit-chat and long decision-making. Let's go before I pass out!" Shaya replied.

The two took off in the direction of the restaurant. As they approached, they saw a sight they had never seen before. The building was long and narrow, and there was a car on the roof for decoration. On another part of the roof, there was a large statue of a cow. They walked inside and saw that the walls were plastered with signed American dollar bills. There was a bar and some random tables throughout the room. "You sure know how to pick 'em!" Jexi said with a snicker.

Shaya elbowed her and replied, "At least if we can't pay for lunch, we can borrow money from the walls."

The hostess met them at the door and asked them if they would prefer to sit inside or outside by the water. "Outside," said the girls simultaneously. The hostess picked up two menus and led them to a table on the waterfront.

Shaya looked over the ledge. "We are literally on the water," she said. She looked at Jexi. "Don't fall in, okay?" she teased.

Jexi harrumphed. "No promises!" she said.

Shaya and Jexi sat down at the table and perused the menus. "What is frikandel?" Jexi asked quizzically.

"I can assure you that I have no idea," Shaya replied. "I am going to stick with something I can pronounce. Like a bacon cheeseburger!"

Jexi looked at her. "That sounds good. But I doubt that it's genuine Aruban cuisine," she laughed.

Shaya snickered, "If it is made in Aruba, it is definitely Aruban food!"

Jexi laughed again. "That is a good theory!"

The server arrived at their table and asked them what they would like to drink. She began listing the several alcoholic drinks that they had on special. Jexi politely stopped her and said, "No, thank you. I'll just have bottled water."

Shaya chimed in, "Same for me, please."

"We are also ready to order," Jexi said. The server pulled out a notepad and a pen. "I will have the bacon cheeseburger."

"Me too," said Shaya. "And a side of fries."

Jexi looked at the server as she handed back the menus. "Um, can you tell us what the frikandel is?" The server held her pen at the ready. "We don't want any, we are just curious about what it is because it is a fun food name."

"It is basically a deep-fried sausage," the waitress explained. "The food is much more boring than its name implies. But it is very delicious."

"Oh, okay!" said Shaya. "Thanks!"

The waitress left to submit their order to the kitchen. Jexi and Shaya talked about their morning and how much fun they'd had. They both said that they looked forward to going to the beach after lunch.

All of a sudden, they heard a voice say, "I would recognize those auburn curls anywhere. Shaya Clark, as I live and breathe!"

Shaya froze and her eyes widened. She slowly turned in the direction from which the voice came. As she saw who was speaking to her, her face blushed red. "Ben?" she quietly asked. "Ben? What the heck?"

Jexi heard the mention of Ben's name and gasped. "Ben?!" she loudly proclaimed. "THE Ben?!"

Shaya looked at her and kicked her under the table. "Yes, Jexi, this is Ben Thatcher." She turned back to Ben and stammered out, "Um, how is it possible that you're here?"

Jexi noticed that there was another man with Ben. He hadn't said anything, but Jexi had a gut feeling that she had seen his face somewhere. "I've seen you before, but I can't remember where," she stated, with a puzzled look on her face. Recognition slowly washed over her as she realized where she had seen him. "Wait! You're that singer from the Gospel Hour!"

The man stretched out his hand and said, "Yes, that's me. My name is Hunter Bennett. Pleased to meet you."

Jexi reached out to shake his hand. She noticed how handsome he was but then immediately dismissed the thought. "I am Jexi Driscoll. Nice to meet you as well."

Shaya was still frozen with shock while Jexi said, "And this one with her jaw on the ground is my best friend, Shaya Clark."

Hunter nodded toward Shaya. "Pleasure," he said. Shaya was staring at Ben in disbelief. The four stood there for several awkward seconds. Hunter stared at the ground as he shuffled his feet.

Ben broke the silence. "Mind if we join you?" he asked.

Jexi stood and took two chairs from the table next to them. "Yes, of course," she said, and she invited the men to sit down. Under her breath, she muttered, "This should be fun." She reached for Shaya's arm and squeezed it.

Shaya snapped out of her stupefaction and stammered, "Oh, yes, um, sure. We have already ordered but let me get our server." She left the table hurriedly and disappeared into the restaurant. When she returned, her pulse had returned to almost normal again. "She is on her way," she announced.

The men sat down at the table and the awkward silence resumed. This time, Hunter spoke to Ben. "So, how do you know these lovely ladies?"

Ben glanced embarrassingly at Shaya and she blushed again. "Um, I've not met Jexi until now, but Shaya and I used to, um, well, we used to date."

Hunter's eyebrows lifted and an exclamation of understanding softly escaped from his lips. "Ohhh, I see."

Shaya's eyes were still laser-focused on Ben and when she found her voice, she asked, "What are you doing here? Why are you in Aruba . . . right now?"

Ben smiled. "I am on our church's worship team with Hunter. I don't usually get on the stage much, I'm more of a behind-the-scenes guy. Most of the time, I help with the equipment and things like that. Hunter is the main scene. Our team got hired to lead the two worship nights on the ship. It is so crazy that we are on the same cruise! I mean, what are the odds? What are you doing here in Aruba?"

The waitress appeared with Shaya and Jexi's water and took Ben and Hunter's orders. They both ordered bottled water and bacon cheeseburgers as well.

When the waitress walked away, Shaya glanced at Jexi. "It is pretty wild, isn't it? Um, Jex, would you like to explain?"

Jexi sat up straight. "Might as well," she said. "We are on my honeymoon," she added matter-of-factly.

Hunter's eyebrows raised again. "Honeymoon? You're married? And you brought your best friend with you? Is your husband okay with that?"

Shaya spoke up, "That is a completely different story. But to make it quick and as painless as possible, it is just me and Jexi. The wedding didn't happen, and we didn't want this amazing trip to go to waste."

Hunter and Ben nodded but didn't know what to say. Jexi looked at the guys. "It's okay," she said. "You don't have to feel sorry for me. I am having a great time with my bestie."

At that moment, the waitress brought their food and the four made small talk while they ate. Shaya and Ben did most of the catching up while Jexi and Hunter listened to them reminisce.

Toward the end of lunch, the guys offered to pay for the girls' meal. They gratefully accepted and talked about what they could do that afternoon.

Ben asked, "Hey, let's go to the beach and swim. The waters here are crystal clear, and I have been itching to go snorkeling!"

Jexi and Shaya agreed since they were already planning to go to the beach anyway. While the men walked to the counter to pay for lunch, the girls excused themselves to the restroom.

Once in the restroom, Shaya let out a huge breath. She turned to Jexi, grabbed her shoulders, and shook them vigorously. "Oh, my goodness," she said. "How is this even happening?"

Jexi pulled away and said, "I don't know, but there is no need to shake my head off my body! Chill out and breathe!"

Shaya shook her again and exclaimed, "But you don't understand! BEN is HERE! Right here! Well, not RIGHT here. He's actually out THERE paying for our lunch. But he is HERE!"

Jexi laughed. "I have never seen you this flustered! You are a mess! Yes, Ben is in Aruba and so are you. This is the wildest coincidence I've ever seen!"

Shaya suddenly dropped her arms and sighed. "It's not a coincidence," she said quietly. "I don't believe in coincidences. God had our paths cross here for a reason. The problem is, I don't know what that reason is just yet."

CHAPTER FIVE

Jexi looked at Shaya. "Well, whatever you call it, he is out there waiting for us. We can't hide in here forever."

Shaya went to the sink and splashed some cool water on her face. "Okay," she said. "I'm ready."

The girls walked out of the bathroom and saw the two guys waiting for them at the entrance of the restaurant. Jexi noticed the way that Ben was gazing at Shaya. There was no mistaking that he was still in love with her. She had seen that same look in Brennan's eyes at one time. She glanced at Shaya. She was beaming. Jexi had never seen her light up so much as she was at that moment. Jexi giggled out loud as she pictured a slow-motion scene where the two are running toward each other in a field of flowers.

The other three turned to look at her as if to ask about what was so funny. "Oh, nothing," she muttered. "Just a funny thought."

"Did you have a particular beach picked out?" Jexi asked the guys.

Ben answered, "No, we aren't really sure which beach we should go to. Did you two have one in mind?"

Shaya shook her head no. "Let's ask the bartender."

Hunter walked to the bar and had a brief conversation with the bartender. He returned to the group. "We can walk ten minutes south to a good beach or we can get a cab and go north to an even better beach."

"Cab it is," said Shaya.

"Okay, I'll hail us one," said Ben. He walked out to the sidewalk, put his hand in the air, and used his other hand to put two fingers in his mouth to whistle. He yelled, "Cab!" He looked back at the group and said with a grin, "I've always wanted to do that!"

The four piled into a car that pulled up and Hunter gave the driver the beach's name. There wasn't a lot of talk on the way to the beach as the group looked out the windows and took in all the sights. When they arrived at the beach, the girls offered to pay for the cabbie. Hunter looked at Jexi and said, "Nah, you've had a hard enough time lately. I'll cover it." He handed some bills to the driver.

The group filed out of the cab and walked down to the beach to find a location that suited them all. They all agreed on a spot not too far from the water and Shaya spread a blanket on the sand.

Jexi immediately dropped her bags in the sand, kicked off her shoes, and waded into the shallow water. It was cool, but not too cold. It felt incredible. She was amazed at how closely the fish swam around her legs. Some even brushed against her feet and tickled her. Right then, she felt a peace that filled her heart. She noticed that it was slightly out of place, compared to what she had been feeling. Could this possibly be the peace that Shaya had told her about? She was utterly transported to a different dimension of emotion. She could have stayed in this place and time forever.

Hunter looked at Ben and Shaya, who seemed to be picking up where they left off years ago. He suddenly felt like a very uncomfortable third wheel. He decided to join Jexi in the water. He walked to where she was standing and said, "Breathtaking, isn't it?"

Jexi turned to him with a big smile on her face. "It is incredible," she replied. "One of the most beautiful things I've ever seen."

Hunter laughed and said, "I noticed you didn't even take time to change into your swimsuit."

Jexi looked down at her clothes, soaked from the knees down. "Oh, yeah, you're right," she giggled. "I guess I was just so excited to get into the water that I didn't even think." She paused and looked back at the beach. "Ah, who cares? They are just clothes after all. They'll dry."

Hunter laughed. "I like your way of thinking." He got a sly smile on his face and bent down. He scooped up a handful of water and splashed it on her.

Jexi squealed with laughter. In an instant, she bent down, following the same process, and splashed him back. She couldn't believe it, but was she having fun?

Hunter pointed out different fishes that could be seen through the water. There were fish of so many different colors! There were also beautiful corals and colorful plants. He was just as amazed as Jexi was at the sight.

As Jexi and Hunter stood talking and goofing around in the crystal-clear water, she thought about how she was actually enjoying herself. She had been thinking that she would just be miserable for the foreseeable future. But here she was, laughing and almost forgetting about Brennan for a moment. She was thankful for the break from reality, and she smiled at Hunter. He smiled back and, for a brief second, she thought she might have felt a slight attraction for him.

She turned away from Hunter and chided herself. Of course, she wasn't attracted to him. She was still in love with Brennan and there might be a chance to get him back. This was just some handsome stranger who she'd never see again after this cruise. She looked at Hunter and said, "I am going to get my swimsuit on. That way I won't have to swim in my clothes."

Hunter laughed. "That sounds like a good plan. I'll get changed too."

The two walked out of the water back to where Shaya and Ben were deep in conversation. Jexi tapped Shaya on the shoulder. "I'm going to get changed into my suit," she said.

Shaya looked up at Jexi and nodded. "I'll change too," she stated.

Ben looked at Hunter. "I suppose we can go get our suits on as well, but you girls go get changed first and we'll stay with the stuff. Then we can go after you."

Shaya and Jexi thanked the guys and walked to the changing house. While they were getting into their swimsuits, Jexi asked Shaya, "Soooo . . . how are things going with Ben?"

Shaya giggled. "Wonderfully!" she responded. "It's like we haven't been apart at all. But I'm extremely confused. He still hasn't told me why he disappeared and why I never heard from him again. I don't know how to ask and I'm almost too scared to bring it up. What if that brings back bad juju?!"

Jexi replied, "I hear you, but you'll never know if you don't ask. Do you think you two are headed toward getting back together?"

Shaya snorted. "Whoa! Slow down! We literally just ran into each other earlier today! We haven't even gotten to the topic of a girlfriend. For all I know, he is in a relationship with some gorgeous blond back home!"

"But you both look so happy to see each other! It doesn't seem awkward at all!" Jexi insisted.

"That's because we haven't talked about the hard stuff yet!" Shaya groaned.

"Want me to ask?" Jexi offered.

Shaya whipped around quickly. "NO!" she screamed. "Do NOT do that! Not yet anyway."

"Just let me know," Jexi snickered.

The girls finished getting their suits on. "Let's go relieve the guys," Shaya said, eager to end the conversation and, if she was honest, eager to see Ben without a shirt.

The two walked back to the blanket on the beach and swapped places with the guys. They sat in silence while they waited for them to return. They enjoyed the sun as it beat down on their bodies, warming them. Jexi wanted to push the topic of Ben but knew Shaya's warning signs when she's had enough and decided to stay quiet for now.

Within moments, Ben and Hunter walked back to the blanket on the beach and Shaya's eyes opened wide and she sucked in a deep breath. Ben was just as handsome as he had always been, maybe even more. But what was she supposed to do? As much as she wanted to, she couldn't deny that she still had strong feelings for him. Standing before her was the only man she had ever loved.

"Let's go swimming! Race you!" Jexi called and took off running to the water. The other three followed, yelling after her and laughing. The group spent ample time swimming around and playing in the ocean. It was the most fun Jexi could ever remember having. How was it possible that THIS was her best day ever and it didn't include Brennan?

After they had swum for a couple of hours, the four sat on the blanket talking. Suddenly Jexi stated, "Hey, guys! I have a great idea! I saw signs for a sunset sailing cruise while we were on our way to the beach. Watching the sunset over the water. Wouldn't that be a perfect way to end this day?"

Shaya glared at Jexi. She had an idea that Jexi was up to something sneaky. But before she could say anything, Ben spoke first. "Yes! That is a great idea! Lead the way!"

Jexi found her phone and looked up the location from where the sunset sailing would be leaving. "We need to get changed quickly," she said. "It leaves in forty minutes. Good thing it's not too far away."

The group gathered their things and headed for the changing houses. Once there, Shaya confronted Jexi. "What are you doing?" she inquired.

Jexi had an innocent look on her face. "Nothing," she insisted. "I just thought that a sailing cruise on the water during sunset would be amazing!"

Shaya rolled her eyes. "And an amazing way to get me and Ben together?" she accused.

Jexi shrugged, "Well, it would be a pretty perfect opportunity, wouldn't it? Plus," she reminded, "What was it you were saying about no coincidences?"

"Shut up," Shaya retorted. She huffed and pretended to be angry with Jexi. Her heart and stomach were filled with butterflies. She felt like she might throw up. But a part of her was excited about the excursion; secretly, she agreed it would be amazing! Shaya also loved that this little match-making plan was making Jexi happy. She wanted to see her best friend happy, after all.

CHAPTER SIX

Once the girls finished changing, they met the guys in front of the changing houses. Jexi spoke up and said, "We just need to head south about a quarter mile."

The group walked to the dock from where the sailing cruise would be departing. They could see several patrons climbing the ramp and loading onto the sailboat. Jexi ran ahead to the attendant at the kiosk to ask about tickets.

"Do we have to have reservations to come on the sunset sail?" she asked.

The attendant shook his head and replied, "No, you don't need to reserve a spot, but we are filling up fairly quickly. Let's get you on this boat!"

Jexi waved the rest of her friends over to her. "We can sail tonight!" she said excitedly.

The others rushed over to the kiosk and each one paid for their own passage. Then they enthusiastically boarded the sailboat and found four seats.

Ben and Shaya sat next to each other, exchanging glances and smiles. Shaya was nervous about what she was feeling toward this beautiful man from her past. The two had done quite a bit of talking that day but Shaya still had so many questions. She really wanted to know why he had just stopped all contact years ago. She wanted to know how he felt about her right now. She wanted to yell at him. She wanted to hug him. But she just could not get her mouth to say anything of significance.

The boat cast off into the late afternoon light and the view was breathtaking, to say the least. The oranges, purples, pinks, and yellows from the beginning of the sun setting streaked across the heavens. The water reflected the light from the sun, and it seemed as if it was covered in diamonds. The sky held a mixture of a darkening blue sky and wispy clouds that soaked up the colors of the sun.

"God's artistry knows no bounds," Ben whispered. "He certainly painted a masterpiece tonight."

In her heart, Shaya marveled at God's handiwork. At that moment, she almost felt that her problems melted away and everything was perfect. In a way, she was glad that she was experiencing this with Ben.

Jexi was taking in the scene with amazement. She once again felt a sense of peace in her heart. It was hard to be angry and bitter while riding the waves of what must have been heaven. As the sun dropped from the sky and into the water, Jexi felt a bit of softening of her heart. She thought again of the peace of God and pondered if this was what she was feeling. But this didn't make sense to her. Why would God bother with reaching out to her when she was so angry at Him? She dropped her head and stared at her hands. Confusion washed through her and she began to feel tears well up in her eyes. She quickly composed herself and looked at the sky again. The colors shifted slightly as the sun set and the beauty was undeniable. She decided to simply enjoy the view and relax.

As twilight took over, Shaya felt someone's hand resting on top of hers. She looked and saw Ben attempting to hold her hand in his. She quickly pulled her hand away and sought to refocus his attention. "Does anyone want appetizers?" she asked as she stood up. "I see some yummy things listed on the menu!" Shaya began walking to the counter.

Jexi and Hunter both stood up. "Yes, I am definitely hungry," Jexi said.

Hunter added, "Me too!" He looked at Ben who remained seated. "You coming, bro?"

Ben stayed in his seat. "Nah," he replied. "You all go on."

Hunter shrugged. "Okay," he replied. "Let's get some grub, girls."

The three walked to the counter. Jexi and Shaya walked just a bit behind Hunter. Jexi leaned over to Shaya and asked, "What is with you? You seem awfully jumpy."

"He tried to hold my hand," Shaya replied.

"Okay, and?" prompted Jexi.

"That's it. He tried to hold my hand," Shaya informed.

"That's IT?!" Jexi hissed. "You're freaking out because he tried to hold your hand?"

"Drop it, Jex. I don't want to talk about this right now," Shaya whispered as they reached the counter.

Hunter, Jexi, and Shaya each placed an order for an appetizer and stood waiting for their food in disquieted silence.

Hunter received his food first and went back to sit with Ben. Jexi began to speak, but before she could say a word, Shaya shot her a look and whispered, "I still don't want to talk about it."

"Fine. But this conversation is definitely NOT over!" Jexi stated with strong conviction.

Shaya rolled her eyes. Her name was called and she collected her food. Jexi wondered what was going on with her best friend. Shaya tells her everything! What was it about Ben that was keeping her so hush-hush? Jexi's name was called, and she took her food back to the group.

The stars were becoming more and more visible as the night overtook daylight. Jexi couldn't be sure, but it almost seemed as if they gleamed brighter here than they did back home. They looked to be so close that she could practically reach out and pluck one from the sky. She took out her phone and opened the camera. She aimed it at the gorgeous scenery and snapped several pictures. "Darn!" she exclaimed, "My phone camera can't seem to capture the enormity of this . . ." Jexi paused. "I can't even find the perfect word! Perhaps I should use a thesaurus." The group laughed and for a brief moment, the tension settled.

"Good luck! We don't have any adequate words to describe the magnificence of God," Shaya stated. "But I know what you mean!"

The four returned to quietness while the cruise began to head back to port. After they had finished eating, Ben leaned over to Shaya and asked, "Can we go somewhere to talk in private?"

Shaya panicked, but managed to stammer out, "Um, yeah, okay, sure."

Ben and Shaya walked to a secluded spot near the railing on the boat. Once he knew they were out of earshot of everyone else, he began. "Shaya, we need to have a serious talk. We both know it. It's been a nice day, but I feel like there is a wall between us and we really need to clear the air."

Shaya turned away from Ben and put her hands on the railing. "Ben, I don't know. I mean, yeah, we have a history, but maybe that's what it should stay, a history."

"Can you just let me in on what's going on with you?" Ben asked. "I've never felt this kind of tension between us before."

"Well, you never ditched me before," Shaya retorted.

"I never ditched you!" Ben exclaimed. "What are you talking about?"

Shaya glared at him. "One minute we are talking practically every day on the phone and then the next minute you stopped calling! I haven't heard from you in years. You don't call that being ditched?"

Ben hung his head. "Well, when you put it that way, I guess you're right."

"I know I'm right!" Shaya quipped back. "I thought we had something and that we were going to," her voice faded, "well, you know."

Ben looked at Shaya, "It's not all on me, though. You had been pulling away for months before that. And you could have called me. Phones work both ways, you know."

"Pulling away?" Shaya asked. "What do you mean?"

"Oh, come on," Ben sighed. "You know exactly what I mean. Every time I called, you were either on your way to study, going to take a test, or even just going out with friends. You didn't have time for me, and I could tell you didn't have room for me in your heart, either."

Shaya spun around to face him. She could feel her blood pulsing. "No room in my heart, Ben? I loved you!"

"How was I supposed to know?" Ben asked. "You never told me that! Plus, at Dad's funeral, when I asked you to stay, you left!"

"You knew I couldn't stay," Shaya stated. "I had to go back to school to finish my finals. I was there on a scholarship and couldn't just walk away!" There was silence between them for a moment.

"But I needed you," Ben said quietly.

Shaya looked at him in disbelief. "What?"

"I needed you," Ben repeated. "I had lost my dad, and my mom was a complete wreck. I was so lost and confused and I needed the one person in my life who I knew I could rely on. Shaya, I loved you. As a matter of fact, I've never stopped loving you."

Shaya felt like she had been slapped. She quickly turned back to the rail and looked out over the stunning scenery until her pulse slowed. "Why didn't you ever say anything? Why didn't you tell me this a long time ago? I had no idea. Ben, I thought you abandoned me and gave up on us without a second thought."

Ben touched Shaya's hand. "I'm sorry," he said. "I wasn't giving up on us. I thought that you were giving up on us and I didn't have the strength to try and save us. It was all I could do to deal with Dad's death."

Tears escaped from Shaya's eyes, though she tried to hold back. "I'm sorry too. I really am. I was so angry with you. But I was just as guilty."

Ben gently placed his hands on her shoulders and turned her to face him. The two gazed at each other for a moment.

"I've missed you," slipped from Shaya's lips. She had been trying so hard to keep her guard up, but with Ben, it was so difficult to do. At that moment, she allowed the pain to slip away and realized what she had always believed to be true. There is no such thing as coincidence. God put Ben in her path on this unexpected journey.

"I've missed you too," Ben whispered. He wrapped his arms around Shaya and pulled her into a huge hug. Shaya reciprocated. She felt warm and safe. She remembered feeling this way with him. Both the feeling and the memory made her smile. As she rested her head on his chest, she wished this feeling would never go away.

Jexi wondered what in the world Ben and Shaya were talking about. She would give anything to be a fly on the wall so she could hear them! As she watched them, she could tell that the conversation was intense.

Hunter spoke up. "Looks like they are having one serious talk over there."

Jexi nodded. "I hope everything is okay. Do you know about their history?"

"Some," Hunter replied. "Ben didn't tell me everything, just that they were pretty serious in high school and college but then they drifted apart. Do you think they are headed for a reconciliation?"

As Jexi watched, she saw Ben pull Shaya in for a hug. She smiled. Her heart leaped for joy for her friend. "I most definitely think they are headed for a reconciliation."

"That's good for them!" Hunter said. "I like a happy ending."

Although Jexi was thrilled for her friend, she felt a pang of jealousy. She also felt a bit irritated at Hunter. Happy endings are for those people like Shaya who deserve them. Obviously, she had done something wrong and wasn't worthy of a happy ending. Oh, well, that's the way the cookie crumbles, isn't it? It's a good thing Shaya couldn't hear her thinking right now.

The sailboat pulled into the port, interrupting everyone's thoughts. Ben and Shaya made their way back to Hunter and Jexi and gathered their belongings. They exited the boat and hailed a cab to return to the cruise ship. During the ride, they discussed how beautiful the sunset had been as well as the stars and moon. They mentioned the good food and friendly staff on the boat. They all agreed that it had been a good day.

Jexi could tell Shaya had been crying but she knew this wasn't the time to ask what had happened. She also noticed that Ben and Shaya were touching hands periodically. Hmmm, this was going to be a great story!

Once back onto the ship and in their cabin, Jexi patiently waited for details as the girls readied themselves for bed. Shaya sensed Jexi's curiosity and promised her the full scoop tomorrow.

"Can you at least tell me if you are getting back together?" Jexi asked, excitedly.

Shaya crawled into bed and pulled up the blanket. "We'll see."

She knew that would drive Jexi crazy but, for the moment, that's all she wanted to share. She wanted to keep the conversation with Ben to herself for just a little longer.

CHAPTER SEVEN

The girls woke up early. Neither of them slept very well. Jexi was filled with anticipation and Shaya spent a lot of the night pondering her future. Though both girls were sleepy-eyed, they were ready to see what today would bring. Shaya caught Jexi up to speed about what was happening between her and Ben while they were preparing for the day. She shared the main highlights but kept some of the more intimate details to herself.

Jexi was excited for Shaya and the possibility that she and Ben might become an item again. She could tell that this was something Shaya really wanted, whether she was willing to admit it or not.

Once they were ready for breakfast, they walked to the buffet. They filled their plates with food and sat down to eat. Shaya asked, "What should we do today?"

"Didn't you make plans with Ben?" Jexi asked.

"No," Shaya replied, "This is our trip, and I am not leaving you out."

Jexi teased Shaya, "Aww, you looooove me! You want to spend time with me!"

"Quit making it weird!" Shaya said with an eye roll.

Jexi giggled. "Too late!"

"Seriously," Shaya said. "What are we going to do today?"

Jexi perked up. "I saw something about horseback riding on the beach in a flyer near Guest Services. What do you think?"

Shaya's eyes widened, "That sounds perfect! Would you believe that's on my bucket list? Let's do it!"

"Are you sure you wouldn't rather spend the day with Ben?" Jexi asked.

"Look, Jex, it would be nice to spend the day with Ben sometime, but right now, I am here with YOU and I don't intend to abandon you on your honeymoon, Shaya said with a sly smile. She hoped Jexi would sense the lighthearted humor and not be hurt by the reminder.

Jexi smiled. "Thanks. I appreciate it."

The two finished their breakfast and walked toward the Guest Services desk to inquire about horseback riding. As they approached the desk, they saw a familiar head of hair on a tall guy in line.

"Hunter," Shaya said, "Is that you?"

Hunter turned around. "In the flesh!" he responded. "What are you two up to?"

Jexi clapped her hands excitedly and jumped up and down. "We're going horseback riding on the beach!" she squealed.

Shaya chimed in, "It's something I've always wanted to do."

Hunter grinned. "That sounds like a lot of fun! Have a great day!" he said.

"Thanks!" sang the girls in unison as Hunter walked away.

Jexi walked to the desk. "We would like to get two tickets to the beach horseback riding, please."

The attendant processed their request on the computer and printed their tickets. "The shuttle leaves from the dock area at ten o'clock. It will take you to the beach for the excursion and then will return to the dock at approximately four o'clock this afternoon. Please make sure to load the shuttle ten minutes early both departing and returning."

"Do we need to take money for lunch?" Shaya asked.

"No," the attendant replied, "lunch is included in the price of the excursion. Don't forget your sunscreen, though. You don't want to spend the rest of the cruise burnt!"

The girls thanked the gentleman and looked at the time. It was currently eight twenty-four. They needed to get to their cabin to pack their bags and fill their water bottles. They also needed to change into appropriate clothing and apply sunscreen.

They scurried back to their cabin to make the needed preparations. They giggled and chattered as they did so. They were both very excited about their adventure.

An hour later, they were at the dock waiting for the shuttle. Jexi looked up and saw Hunter and Ben walking toward them. She elbowed Shaya and whispered, "Shaya. Look!"

Shaya looked in the direction Jexi was directing with her eyes. Her heart skipped a beat when her eyes landed on the intended target. She could not deny what she was feeling, but she wasn't quite ready to define it yet.

"Hello, girls!" said Hunter. "Nice to see you again!"

"What are you two doing?" asked Jexi.

Ben answered her, "We are going horseback riding on the beach. Hunter told me that you two are going on the same trip. How uncanny!" He winked at Shaya.

Shaya felt herself smile and blush a little. "You're going on this one too? Did you decide to do this after Hunter told you we were going?"

"Actually, no," replied Ben. "We had already made the plans for this excursion. Hunter was just picking up our tickets this morning."

Shaya's heart was doing flips inside her chest while she did her best to maintain her outward composure. She was so glad that she and Ben were going to be able to spend more time together. She said a silent prayer of thanks to God.

Jexi had mixed emotions. She enjoyed Hunter's company; he was a nice guy. But she had been looking forward to spending time with Shaya. She also wanted Shaya to be happy and she could clearly see that Ben made her extremely happy. So, she set her mind to have a great day. She did, however, find it a strange coincidence that for the past two days, these men always seemed to be where she and Shaya were.

She knew that Shaya didn't believe in coincidences. Could this have been something more? Divine intervention? She shook her head. Nah, it was simply a coincidence. Although she did admit it was an odd one.

The shuttle arrived and they all climbed on the open-window bus. The seats were all cracked, and the bus creaked as if it had been used for decades. The driver smiled at them as they boarded, and Jexi noticed that he was missing a few teeth.

They found seats on the bus and attempted to have conversations as the bus traveled to the beach. However, the bus' engine was too loud and no one could hear any of the others, so they gave up on talking.

They arrived at a ranch about forty minutes later and were shown to the stables. There, several guides talked with different guests about their riding skills and abilities and provided them with the gear they would need. After talking with Jexi, she was chosen to ride a brown horse named Grace. Shaya's horse was named Mercy, and she was all white with the longest mane Jexi had ever seen.

Hunter was paired with a brown-and-white steed named Moses and Ben's black-and-white horse was named King. The group was given a small crash course in mounting and handling the quirks of their assigned horses. Then they all got onto their horses and the ride began.

Shaya and Jexi both had their phones out and were taking numerous pictures. On one side, the clear blue ocean waves rolled into the sandy beach. The water went as far as their eyes could see and seemed to touch the sky. The other side was filled with an incredible amount of beautiful green! Everything was green, except the tree trunks and an occasional bunch of brightly colored flowers. Jexi remembered Ben's comments from the previous night and thought to herself that this was another example of God's artistry. Even though she didn't understand God, she did believe in Him and had to agree that He was quite the painter.

The girls were having a wonderful time talking and laughing with each other as well as Hunter and Ben. The horses were gentle and rhythmic. The girls were getting to know their horses' personalities as they rode. Jexi found it interesting that the horses knew exactly where to go and stayed with the group on their own. She didn't even need to hold the reins to guide her.

There was also plenty of time for thinking. Jexi pondered the names of the horses. She found it curious that they all seemed to have a name associated with Christianity. Again, she found that to be an odd coincidence. Her horse, Grace, seemed to embody the meaning of her name, being very sweet and loving. Jexi discovered that scratching her behind the ears would make her whinny approvingly. She enjoyed the sound of the horse's happiness, so she scratched her often.

An hour later, they arrived at a natural swimming pool where they stopped to have lunch and do some swimming. It was extremely hot, so Jexi welcomed the idea of heading into the water.

"Are y'all hungry?" Jexi asked. "Or would you like to swim first?"

Shaya pointed at the clear water in the natural pool. "I'm sweating and that water looks so refreshing," she said. "I vote to start with a dip!"

Ben immediately supported Shaya by saying, "I vote for swimming too!"

Hunter shrugged his shoulders and said, "I could stand to cool off a bit before lunch."

"I have an idea," Shaya announced, "Let's take the horses into the water. They are hot too! Please, please, can we?"

Jexi nodded, "Yeah, Grace seems like she might need to cool off too. Let's do it!"

Hunter looked over at one of the guides, "Excuse me, sir, can we take the horses into the water?"

The guide said, "Why, yes, of course; the horses love that very much."

The four turned their horses into the cool water and the horses splashed around in the pool. Jexi thought it was silly that the horses seemed to be playing in the water by lifting a leg and splashing repeatedly. The four of them were quickly getting soaked! It was one of the most fun experiences she could remember. She was too high up to reach the water, but she felt a strong urge to splash Shaya. She slipped one foot out of the stirrup and stretched her toes toward the water. When she made contact, she swung her leg toward Shaya. Her quick movement startled Shaya's horse to move and she ended up splashing Hunter instead. Hunter laughed as his horse swished his tail, flinging water all over Jexi.

"Hey!" Jexi screamed.

Hunter laughed, "I didn't do it! Moses has a mind of his own. He has experience with parting water, you know," he teased back.

They ventured out a little deeper at the suggestion of one of the guides. It was a little scary to take the horses out into the vast ocean but, surprisingly, the horses were not scared. When they reached deep water, the horses lifted their hooves and began to swim. Jexi and Shaya looked at each other in amazement. This had to be the coolest thing ever.

As the horses swam, Jexi could feel the water rising on her thighs. Even though she was an experienced swimmer, she became a bit uneasy. Sensing her nervousness, Hunter comforted her by saying, "Trust the horses. They know what to do. They were trained for such a moment as this. Better yet, trust God. He is in control. He will take care of us."

Jexi grunted quietly. There he goes again. Talking about God. Does God even care about me right now? Is He keeping us safe? She closed her eyes for a moment and felt Grace underneath her, kicking, swimming, strong and confident. She felt a warm breeze across her face. She seemed to hear a faint whisper saying that everything was okay. Jexi allowed herself to listen to Hunter's words and she felt the sense of unease melt away.

After a bit, they guided the horses back to shore so they could eat lunch. They dismounted in the way that they were taught before they departed and loosely tied their horses' reins to posts. They dried off as best as they could and went to see what options there were for lunch.

Jexi was surprised at how much food the restaurant had available. Three tables at least four feet long each were placed end to end and packed with food. The buffet options seemed endless. The four grabbed plates and silverware and dove into a fabulous lunch.

After lunch, they were all so full, they could barely move. They went to sit down in some of the lounge chairs under the umbrellas near the pool. Jexi was so exhausted that she quickly laid back, shut her eyes, and fell asleep. Hunter also laid back and dozed off. Ben and Shaya talked for a few minutes, but soon, they too were snoozing in their lounge chairs.

Ben woke up first and looked at his watch. He realized that they would be leaving the area in about thirty minutes. He gently called to the others to rouse them.

"Hey, guys, we are leaving in about thirty minutes," Ben said. "Do you think we have time for another swim?"

Shaya sat up quickly. "I'm in!" she said.

Hunter sat up rubbing his eyes. "What do you think, Jexi? Want to go swimming?"

Jexi watched Hunter stretch and thought about how he had helped her calm down before. He was just such a nice guy. Or, was she just feeling vulnerable? Oh, well, she didn't need to figure it all out right now. Now was a good time for swimming!

"Yep!" she replied. "Let's go!"

The four jumped back into the natural pool and played around for a little while longer. Jexi began to feel like a child again, playing with her friends. She remembered feeling this happy when she was growing up and she remembered feeling this happy planning a life with Brennan. Darn! She hadn't thought about him in hours! She threw the thoughts of him out of her mind and focused on the great time she was having at the moment. He had ruined enough of her life. She didn't want to let him ruin anymore.

CHAPTER EIGHT

The ride back to the stables seemed to take forever. Jexi was completely worn out from the spectacular adventure. Having Hunter and Ben tag along had been unexpected, but if Jexi was honest, they had made the day even more memorable.

Once back at the stables, the group dismounted the horses, gathered their belongings, and then boarded the shuttle bus. Between the loudness of the bus and the group being exhausted, there was not a lot of talking on the way back.

"Nap time!" Jexi announced as they exited the bus.

"You already had a nap!" Shaya reminded her.

"Maybe, but one can never have too many naps," Jexi responded.

Shaya laughed. They walked to the ship and stood in the hallway to say goodbye to the boys.

"I hear there is a good band playing tonight," Ben said with a grin.

Hunter winked. "Yeah! I've heard of those guys! They are supposed to be spectacular!"

"They are okay, I guess," Shaya added.

Jexi giggled. She knew that Shaya was already planning on going to see the guys play. As they departed from Hunter and Ben, she thought about her options for the evening. She could go with Shaya to the worship night, or she could stay in the cabin and read. As uncomfortable as she felt the last time, she was more inclined to stay in the cabin. She wished she had something to read besides that ridiculous predictable lovey-dovey novel.

Back at the cabin, after a brief nap, the girls took some time to call their families back home to let them know that everything was going smoothly, and they were safe.

"I've been so worried," Jexi's mom said to her. "I was wondering how you would do on this trip. Maybe you shouldn't have gone."

"Mom, I'm fine," Jexi reassured her. "I've actually had some fun! Don't worry about me!" There was a short pause. Then Jexi asked, "Um, has anyone seen Brennan?"

Jexi's mom snorted. "He better pray I don't see him!" she yelled. "Otherwise, he'll be buried in my flower bed!"

"Mawm," Jexi pleaded, "Don't be like that. I was just, you know, curious. It's probably best no one has seen him anyway. I mean, what would y'all say?"

Jexi finished the call with her mother assuring her that she really was doing just fine. "I promise, Mom. Shaya is taking good care of me. Give Dad my love. I'll call again in a couple of days."

The girls weren't incredibly hungry because of the big lunch they had, but they decided to go to dinner to see what they could grab to munch on. They went to the daily restaurant and sat down to eat a small meal. "I noticed you didn't mention Ben to your mom when you called her," Jexi stated.

Shaya rolled her eyes at Jexi. She was doing a lot of that on this trip. "What is it with you?" she asked. "Why are you pestering me about this?"

"I just want to know if you guys are getting back together. Clearly, you are smitten with each other! I can see it when I look at you both. Besides, I'm your best friend! We share everything. Certainly, you need to process all of this! Why can't you admit that you still love him?"

"Fine! Yes, I still love him," Shaya said. Jexi started to respond but Shaya continued, "BUT I am not going to rush into anything without spending a considerable amount of time in prayer about my decision.

NEW BEGINNINGS—NOT MY WILL • 49

I don't want to jump into something before asking God's will on my life."

Jexi replied, "I know you have a good head on your shoulders and you'll make the right decision. You always do! I don't know how you do it, to be honest!"

"Lots of prayer," Shaya responded.

Jexi stared at her. "You really mean that, don't you?"

"Absolutely!" Shaya stated. "I submit to God's guidance and the best way to hear Him is through prayer."

"Hear Him?" asked Jexi. "Now you've got me confused. How can you hear God? I've never heard Him speak." But as she was saying the words, she remembered feeling like she heard a voice earlier that day on the horse.

Shaya looked as if she had been prepared for this moment for a long time. "Jexi, I know you're mad at Him. And I understand why. I've been mad at Him too. But that is different from turning away from Him. It's okay to tell Him that you're angry."

Jexi looked skeptical. "Tell Him?" she asked. "I believe in God but all this talk about hearing Him and telling Him is a little too much to grasp."

"Think of Him like your best friend," Shaya answered. "You talk to me, and hear me, right? It's basically the same thing. The difference is that we don't always hear an audible voice from God."

"Then how do you know it's Him?" Jexi asked.

"The more time I spend in prayer and seeking His will, the more I know His voice," Shaya said. "Sometimes it's a song, sometimes it's a feeling, sometimes it's through a friend and many more different ways. You get to a place where you just KNOW."

"Okay, okay . . . this is way over my head now," Jexi said. Shaya sensed from her friend that this was as far as this conversation was going to go right then.

"It's okay. We can talk more some other time. For now, are you going to come with me to worship tonight?" Shaya asked.

Jexi thought about the one and only book she brought to read. She thought also about seeing her best friend's eyes twinkle when she looked at Ben. She also was not opposed to seeing Hunter again. "Sure, I'll go with you. What time does the music start?"

"It starts at eight. Same room as last time," Shaya replied.

"Okay. I'm going to go for a short walk and I'll meet you there. Is that cool?" Jexi suggested.

Shaya was ecstatic that Jexi was going to the worship night and she couldn't help but smile. "Of course!" she answered. "I'll see you then!"

Jexi smiled. "See you then!" she said as she started to walk away.

Shaya hollered after her, "Don't you ditch out on me!"

Jexi yelled back, "I won't! I promise!"

Jexi walked to one of the decks on the side of the ship. The sun was setting, and the breeze was gentle. She stood at the railing looking at the water being churned up by the ship. She noticed a couple several feet away hugging and sharing kisses. She felt a sharp pang in her gut. That should have been her and Brennan. But it wasn't. He didn't want her. Darn him, anyway. What went wrong? How had her life gotten so off track? She reviewed the events of the wedding that never happened in her mind. Had it really only been five days ago? She was able to remember things a little bit more clearly now. He told her that he thought he was ready for marriage but that he was wrong. Why did he wait so long to tell her that? Had she done something wrong? She had so many questions.

Suddenly, she felt a warm breeze, similar to the one she felt earlier that day. It was calming in an inexplicable way. She couldn't understand why she felt peace in that breeze. Peace. There it was again. Here was all this turmoil with Brennan but that breeze was giving her peace. It was way too weird! Could Shaya be right? Should she pray and talk to God? What could it hurt?

She looked around her. Good, she was alone. She suddenly felt foolish. She hadn't prayed in years. She wasn't sure that she even remembered how. But, she thought again, What could it hurt?

She clasped her hands and bowed her head. Jexi began, "God, it's me, Jexi. Um, hi. Shaya told me that she prays to You a lot and that I can hear You too. I don't really know what I am doing, but if You are there, and if You do care, would You help me?"

Meanwhile, Shaya busied herself with a little window shopping before worship would begin. She found herself talking to God and asking Him to give her the right words to help Jexi. There were more conversations over the last few days than she and Jexi had ever had about God. Did she say the right things to open the door? "God, may Your spirit move in Jexi and give her the peace and understanding she craves."

Shaya made her way to the entertainment room and found two seats in the front row. She wanted to get close enough to see Ben backstage during worship. She also thought it might be more powerful for Jexi to be close to the front, away from all of the distractions. Surely Jexi could find her since it wasn't too crowded.

Shaya prayed one more time, "God, show her the way. Not my will, not her will, but Your will."

Jexi felt tears burning her eyes. "God, I don't know why all of this has happened. I am scared, sad, hurt, and angry. Shaya says You care about me. If You do, why did You let Brennan do that to me? I can't believe that being stood up at the altar is Your will for anyone. But I can't ignore the feelings I've had the past few days. Has that been You, God?" Jexi pounded her fists on the railing. "Where are You?!" she yelled as tears spilled down her cheeks.

Once again, the breeze blew over Jexi's face. She lifted her head and looked into the sky. "Is that You, God?" she whispered. Somewhere, deep in her heart, a flicker of peace was born.

Jexi felt her phone buzz and she looked. Shaya had texted her, "Where are you?" Six minutes past eight. Oh, no! She was late for the worship, and she promised Shaya she would be there. She started to run but then abruptly stopped. She turned toward the sky. "God, I don't know if that was You, but if it was, thank You." She then turned back and rushed to the worship room.

CHAPTER NINE

Shaya looked at her watch. Ten minutes after eight. Where was Jexi? She had promised that she would show up! Shaya briefly worried that Jexi had changed her mind. She had seemed a little off-center at dinner earlier. She frowned. Had she pushed her too far?

Jexi paused at the door, looking for Shaya. Hunter had already started singing and the lights were dim. Jexi squinted and scanned the room. Then she saw her in the front row. Seriously, Shaya? The front row? She slowly and quietly made her way to the empty seat next to Shaya. Shaya's eyes were closed, so she didn't notice Jexi.

Jexi didn't want to bother her. She seemed to be so content. Jexi turned her attention to Hunter singing. Ben was with him on stage tonight. He'd mentioned that he does that sometimes. They looked so at ease with each other, singing and worshipping. As she listened, she noticed that Hunter had an incredible voice. She hadn't really paid attention to his voice the last time. But she couldn't help but admit that he had a real talent.

Just like last time, the lyrics to the songs were on the screen. Jexi decided to start singing along. She didn't sing very loudly, but she did join in. For some reason, there was something about the people in this room. They were different. They seemed happy and relaxed. Almost as if they didn't have any problems at all. Jexi found herself longing to have what they had. She just wasn't sure what that was.

Shaya must have heard her singing because she turned slowly toward her and smiled. Jexi shrugged in a silent apology and Shaya leaned over to bump Jexi's shoulder with her own. All seemed perfect and right.

Shaya turned back to face the stage. She lifted her arms in the air and began to sing loudly. Jexi couldn't help but giggle at the sight. She decided to lift her voice a little louder and found herself having a really good time! She closed her eyes to let it all sink in and heard a voice say, "I see you. I am with you."

Jexi popped her eyes open and looked around. Everyone was singing and no one appeared as if they had been speaking to her. The only one nearby was Shaya, and she whispered to her, "Why are you being weird? Of course, you are with me."

Shaya stopped singing and looked at her, "What are you talking about? I didn't say anything," she replied.

Jexi froze. "Then who said that?" she asked.

"I didn't hear anything," Shaya said as she went back into worship mode.

That was so strange! Jexi thought to herself. She stood still for a moment. Certainly, it hadn't been . . . no, of course not. But she had heard something. "God, was that you?" she whispered.

The evening progressed quickly, and Jexi was surprised when Hunter announced they were going to pray before their final song for the night. She bowed her head and listened to his prayer. She liked the way his prayer words flowed seamlessly. Her prayer earlier was so mixed up and choppy. She was pretty sure she confused God with her rambling. Maybe she would try again another time.

Hunter finished his prayer by saying, "In Jesus' name we pray, Amen." Jexi would have to ask Shaya about that later. Jexi kept her eyes closed as Hunter and Ben began the last song. As she listened to the music, the lyrics to the song grabbed hold of Jexi's heart and squeezed. She felt the guys were singing directly to HER. What was happening? She wanted to open her eyes, but something compelled her to keep them closed and just listen. The song talked about how

God was holding her. And if she was honest, it was almost as if she could feel some arms embracing her.

She stood still and simply enjoyed the feeling. The song ended and she slowly opened her eyes. She looked at Shaya and Shaya smiled at her.

"Are you okay?" Shaya asked.

"Um, yeah, I am," Jexi replied. "That was a nice evening. And Ben sure looked good up there! Am I right?"

Shaya rolled her eyes, but admitted, "Yes, he sure did! I had no idea he could sing like that. We need to find the guys. I want to tell them how well they did."

"Have the two of you talked about things since the sunset cruise?" Jexi asked.

"No, not really," Shaya answered. "Today was so much fun, but there really wasn't a good time to talk, ya know. Maybe we can talk tomorrow."

Jexi nodded. "Wanna go see if the guys want to get ice cream?"

Shaya grinned sheepishly. "Yeah, I kinda do," she admitted.

Jexi jumped up and down and clapped her hands. "Yay!" she squealed.

The girls saw Hunter and Ben coming from behind the stage. They waved at them, and the guys walked over to them.

"Great set!" Shaya said, beaming.

"Yeah!" Jexi added. "You both did very well!"

"Thanks," the boys said simultaneously.

"Want to go get ice cream?" Jexi asked.

Ben laughed and looked at his watch, "Ice cream at nine forty at night?"

"That's what I love about a cruise. You can eat all day and all night," Shaya responded.

Hunter chimed in. "Ain't that right?! I'm game!"

The four walked toward the small ice cream shop on board. They each ordered and then found a table to sit down and talk. They all reflected upon the day.

"I am exhausted, but today has definitely been one of my top five all-time best days," said Ben.

Hunter laughed. "Yeah, it certainly was a fabulous day. I mean, horseback riding on a beach, amazing company, and topping the day off with an incredible worship session. Doesn't get much better than this!"

"Don't forget the ice cream!" Jexi piped up.

Shaya smiled and looked at the others. "I have to agree that today was one of the best days I've ever had." As she glanced Ben's way, he winked at her, and it sent a shiver down her spine.

Jexi yawned. She put down her ice cream bowl and licked her lips. "I am wiped. It's time for this girl to hit the hay."

Shaya finished the last bite of her ice cream and stood up. "Same here! Guys, thank you for a memorable day!"

Ben stood up and asked, "Are you sure you have to go?"

Shaya nodded as she yawned, "Yeah, I am so tired. I have got to get some rest. We will talk tomorrow, don't worry."

Ben cocked his head to the left. "Breakfast?" he inquired.

Shaya glanced at Jexi. Jexi nodded. "Yes," Shaya said. "Breakfast. See you in the buffet line at eight."

Jexi saw Ben's face light up with a huge smile. There was no hiding how he was feeling, that was for sure. She looked at Hunter and felt like she should say something, but wasn't sure what. So, she just said, "Good night, y'all!"

The girls walked toward the elevator. "Perhaps we should take the stairs since we just had late-night ice cream," Shaya stated. "I can feel those calories headed straight to my hips!"

"Ugh!" Jexi replied. "How about we take the stairs tomorrow? I don't think I have the stamina to make it up the stairs. I'm practically crawling as it is."

Shaya smiled at her friend. "Okay, you win. We will take the elevator. But it's all stairs tomorrow!"

"You are so bossy!" Jexi said with a laugh.

The girls entered their cabin and began the process of getting ready for bed.

"Guess we need to get some beauty sleep if we're meeting them for breakfast tomorrow, huh?" Jexi mentioned.

Shaya mumbled, "Um hmm," but wasn't fully present in the moment. Her mind was on Ben. She was thrilled at seeing him again. She was so glad that they had cleared the air about their breakup. But she was worried about what the future held. They lived in different cities and the last time they tried a long-distance relationship it hadn't worked out very well. She really wanted the two of them to be together, but was there a practical way that they could make it work?

The girls shut out the lights and Shaya quickly drifted off to sleep. It wasn't as easy for Jexi. She had so much on her mind. Jexi wasn't sure what had happened today, but she felt different somehow. She didn't feel as if the whole world was collapsing on her. She looked at the ceiling of their cabin as if she was looking into the sky. Had God really shown up today? Had He actually been that small voice that she'd heard? She closed her eyes, hoping that sleep would find her. As she crossed into a deep slumber, she heard "I've got you. Rest, my daughter."

CHAPTER TEN

Jexi must have been more tired than she thought because she awoke to Shaya opening and slamming drawers. She groaned and looked at Shaya. "What's with all the noise?" she asked. "It's so early!"

"It's already seven!" Shaya shrieked. "And I can't find the right thing to wear!"

Jexi rolled her eyes. "Seriously?" she asked. "You're panicking about what to wear? You aren't the type to worry about that stuff. Who are you and what have you done with Shaya?" Then understanding washed over her as she became more alert and remembered they were meeting the guys for breakfast. "Ooooohhh, I know," she smirked. Shaya shot her a death glare. "Shut up," she said. "Don't even start."

"Shaya's in love!" Jexi teased. "It's totally fine, Shaya! You could probably wear a gunny sack and Ben would think you looked like a queen. Have you seen how he gushes over you?"

Shaya picked up a shirt and threw it at Jexi, hitting her square in the face. "GET UP! We need to get going."

"Geez!" Jexi grumbled. "Panic much?" She got out of bed and reached into Shaya's closet and casually pulled out a bubblegum pink overall short romper. "Wear this," she said as she handed it to Shaya.

"Yeah, well . . . that's fine but I still need a shirt," Shaya said as her pulse slowed a bit.

"Where is the white shirt you wear with those?" Jexi asked. "Oh, yeah, you THREW it at me." Jexi balled up the shirt and threw it back to Shaya.

"Be careful!" Shaya yelled. "You'll wrinkle it!"

Jexi shook her head and laughed at her friend's frenzied state of mind. She stepped into the bathroom and brushed her teeth. She put on her makeup and then walked to her closet to find something to wear. She didn't want to say anything to Shaya, but secretly she was looking forward to seeing Hunter again. There was something about him that was just comforting. But she was certainly NOT interested in him.

Shaya finished getting ready and stood at the cabin door tapping her foot. "Come on already!" she demanded. "It's already five till!"

"Look, lady," Jexi replied. "Cool your jets, or we will have our first fight. It won't hurt anything to be a minute or two late. Plus, I've never seen you this uptight before! And that is saying something!"

"I know. I'm sorry. I don't know what's wrong with me today. Maybe I didn't get enough sleep," Shaya said. She took a deep breath and let it out slowly. "Okay, I'm all better."

Jexi grinned slyly. "I know what's going on with you. Someone is in looooovve!" She ran out of the cabin door before Shaya could punch her in the arm.

The girls walked to the breakfast buffet and saw Hunter and Ben in the distance. Shaya's heart started doing flips again as soon as she saw Ben. What was it about this man that could do this to her? She was not ready for these feelings. She just wasn't.

Hunter waved. "Hi, ladies!" he said enthusiastically. "How did you all sleep? You both look lovely and refreshed."

Jexi blushed. Immediately she became aware of her blushing and found it to be odd. Why would she blush at Hunter's compliment? She put it out of her mind and smiled. "Thank you," she said. "I know I slept well!"

Shaya looked at Ben and smiled. "I slept well too," she said. "I'm also very hungry!"

Ben smiled back at her. "I am starved," he said. "Let's jump in line. It's been ten hours since my last meal. I don't want to wither away."

Jexi laughed. "Just like a growing boy," she commented. "Always hungry!"

Hunter chuckled. "Us men are always hungry," he responded. "Gotta stay strong and healthy!"

Shaya laughed. "And yet they never gain any weight. It's just not fair!"

The four got into the buffet line and began piling food onto their plates. Jexi was surprised at how easy it was to be with this group. She could be herself, without judgment. She liked that.

"Man, this looks delicious!" Ben exclaimed.

"It has been delicious each morning," said Shaya. "This cruise food has NOT disappointed!"

They found a table for the four of them and they all sat down. Over breakfast, Jexi noticed that Shaya and Ben kept exchanging small glances. They even held hands for a short moment. She thought it was so sweet that they had found each other again. She was so happy for her friend. She couldn't help but think that if she had been on this cruise with Brennan, Shaya would not have been here for this reunion. Was that fate? Coincidence? She knew what Shaya would say.

Hunter asked the girls, "What are your plans for the day?" Shaya and Jexi looked at each other. "We really hadn't thought about it," admitted Jexi. "We are planning on the formal night dinner, but beyond that, we don't know."

Ben spoke up, "There is mini golf on one of the upper decks. Would you two be interested in that?"

"YES!" Jexi exclaimed. "I love mini golf. And I have to say, I'm pretty good at it. In fact, some people might say I excel at mini golf."

"That's big talk for such a little girl." Hunter teased as he stood.

Jexi tilted her head to look up at him. "Is that a challenge?" she asked.

Hunter laughed. "Well, if you put it that way, then yes! I happen to be the mini golf pro of our hometown!"

Shaya looked at Jexi. That smile. She had seen something like it before, but this time it seemed different. Was Jexi developing feelings for Hunter? No, that's unlikely, thought Shaya. She is just enjoying herself right now. That's all. That's a good thing.

The crew of four finished breakfast and made their way to the mini golf area. They selected their putters and golf balls and walked to the first hole.

"Ready for a whoopin'?" Jexi teased Hunter.

"I was going to ask you the same thing," Hunter replied. "I hope you can handle getting beaten this badly." He winked.

Jexi lowered an eyebrow. "Maybe we should make a small wager on the game?" she asked.

Hunter also lowered an eyebrow. "Sounds intriguing. What are the stakes you have in mind?"

"Loser buys the winner a souvenir from the shops. Ten-dollar limit," Jexi countered.

"Just ten dollars? You sound scared. Are you worried you might lose?" Hunter teased.

"Not at all," Jexi stated. "I am just trying to take it easy on you. And when you buy my souvenir, try to remember that I don't need any more key chains." She whisked past Hunter, set her ball down on the tee, and took her first stroke.

"This could be an intense game," Shaya quipped.

They all watched as the ball rolled down the course, bounced off the board in the corner, and headed toward the hole.

Ben said, "Ooooh, Hunter, you may have met your match!" as the ball sank into the hole.

Shaya and Jexi high-fived each other. Shaya grinned. "Yeah, I may have forgotten to tell you that Jexi was on the golf team in college." Jexi tossed an accomplished smile at Hunter and twirled around toward the next hole.

Hunter turned to Shaya with a look of feigned betrayal on his face. "Yeah, you could have mentioned that beforehand," he commented. "But no worry, I too have had some success in the mini-golf arena."

Hunter stepped up to the tee, set down his ball, and began preparing for his first stroke. He took a few practice swings and let out a big sigh. Just as he lifted his club to swing, Jexi whispered loudly to Shaya, "We're about to see if he's as good as he claims."

Hunter's club came down on the golf ball, but when it struck, the ball only made it to the board in the corner and bounced backward.

Shaya and Jexi burst into laughter. "Nice shot!" Shaya teased.

Hunter pointed at Jexi. "She broke my concentration," he complained.

Ben patted Hunter on the back. "There is no shame in losing to a pretty lady," he commented, snickering.

Hunter puffed up his chest. "It's okay," he said. "It's only the first hole. I have seventeen more."

Ben motioned to the tee. "Ladies first," he said to Shaya.

Shaya walked to the tee. "Thank you," she replied. She put her ball on the tee and took her first shot. She swung too hard, and her ball hit the boundary wall and jumped into the green of the neighboring hole. "Oops!" She exclaimed, "I, however, am NOT a skilled golfer."

Ben put his arm around her shoulders and gave her a squeeze. "It's okay," he said. "I'm not very good either."

Shaya shuddered from his touch. How in the world is this man making my knees go weak? she thought. She quickly pulled away from his grasp. "It's your turn," she said softly.

Ben looked hurt by her abrupt escape, but he smiled and stepped up to the tee without a word. He hit the ball with minimal effort, which caused it to roll a few feet down the green slowly.

The next few holes went by quickly as the four laughed and teased each other. Jexi and Hunter were both doing well and had impressive scores.

As they approached the twelfth hole, Jexi and Hunter had a tied score. Shaya and Ben had stopped taking their scores because they both took so many strokes on each hole. They were just playing for fun.

Jexi looked at Hunter and said, "I'm impressed! You are better than I thought you would be."

Hunter grinned. "Thanks! Does this mean that you are accepting that I will win?"

Jexi scoffed. "Oh, my, not in a million years! I am very confident in my game."

The twelfth hole had a small bridge in the middle of the fairway. Jexi noticed that if she hit that bridge square on, she would have an automatic hole-in-one. She concentrated on the spot on the putter where she would need to hit the ball and lifted her club for the swing. She hit the ball with just the right amount of force and the ball rolled over the bridge and straight into the hole.

Jexi jumped in the air. "Hole-in-one! Hole-in-one!" she shouted.

Hunter smirked. "Too easy," he said. He placed his ball on the tee and took his swing. Just exactly as Jexi's ball had done, his ball rolled over the center of the bridge into the hole.

Jexi had to admit to herself that this guy was just as skilled as she was with his golf game. And if she was honest, she liked that about him.

The group moved on through the next five holes. They soon arrived at the eighteenth hole and the score between Jexi and Hunter was still tied.

"This is the deciding hole," said Hunter. "This is where you will meet your defeat."

This hole was definitely the most difficult of the entire course. If a player made it past the windmill, there were two hills that the ball needed to go over. Once the ball made it over the two hills, the player would need to putt the ball into a loop that would take the ball directly into the hole. If the player missed the loop, it would require more shots to go around to fall into the hole.

Jexi took a deep breath and walked to the tee. She calmly set her ball down, but inside she felt nothing but butterflies. Man, it sure would be embarrassing to lose, she thought. She swung her club, and the ball missed the windmill blade and rolled over the first hole. It came to rest in between the two hills. "Bummer," she muttered.

Hunter wanted to gloat, but he refrained and simply walked to the tee. He set his ball down and watched the windmill to time his shot just right. He swung his club, and everyone watched as his ball rolled toward the windmill, bounced off the blade, and rolled all the way back to the tee.

"Heh, heh, heh," Hunter tried to laugh off his mistake.

"It's okay, Hunter," said Jexi with a smug look. "If you need help with picking out my souvenir, my favorite color is purple." She felt better about her first shot and started to think that she could actually win.

Hunter looked at Ben and Shaya who just shrugged their shoulders. Ben gave him a thumbs-up and said, "Try again, buddy. You can do it!"

Hunter looked at the windmill and watched the rhythm that the blades moved in. He struck his ball, and it flew through the mouth of the windmill and over the first hill. It came to rest right next to Jexi's golf ball.

Jexi stepped up to the ball for her second shot. At this point, she was only one stroke ahead of him, which didn't ease her nerves much. She needed to get the ball over the second hill and into that loop. She positioned herself and struck her ball. She watched in dismay as the ball rolled just slightly to the right of the loop. Oh, great, she thought. There go my chances of winning. What is wrong with me today?

Hunter sucked in his breath. "Oh, that's too bad, Jexi! I was sort of rooting for ya. But when you're buying my souvenir, try to remember that I don't need any more mugs."

Jexi tried to pretend that she wasn't upset about the possibility of losing. "You've played a good game, Hunter. But it isn't over yet!"

Hunter walked to his ball and aimed for the loop. "It might not be over yet, but it will as soon as I make this shot," he gloated. Hunter swung his club and hit the golf ball. The ball rolled as if it was headed directly toward the loop and Hunter smiled in triumph. He raised his arms in preparation for a victory cheer. But in a cruel twist of fate, his ball began to swerve slightly to the left.

Jexi couldn't help but let out a holler of delight. She didn't realize that she had been holding her breath while Hunter took his turn. She whooped in laughter as the ball bounced off the left side of the loop and ricocheted to the left wall.

"I'm still one stroke ahead!" Jexi boasted. She walked to her ball and surveyed the situation. Her ball had landed at an awkward angle in relation to the hole. It could take her two shots to get this done unless she reached down deep and tapped into the skills she learned in college. She readied her club and began to swing. She needed a certain amount of force to get this ball to the hole; not too much, not too little. As she brought her club down, she concentrated to make sure she hit the ball just hard enough in the right direction. She made contact with the ball and stood back to see if she had judged the shot correctly.

All of them watched Jexi's ball as it sailed toward the hole. Shaya whispered, "Go in, go in, go in!" Out of excitement, she didn't even notice herself reaching for Ben's hand.

Ben was startled at Shaya grasping his hand, but he didn't say anything. He just held her hand. He didn't even complain when she squeezed it tighter and tighter.

Hunter's heart sank as he watched the golf ball drop flawlessly into the hole. He knew right then that he had lost. He walked to Jexi and extended his hand. "Congratulations," he complimented.

Jexi shook his hand. "Thanks!" she replied. "That was fun!"

Hunter smiled. He did have a good time and, secretly, he was looking forward to getting Jexi a gift.

Shaya wanted to clap for Jexi, but all of a sudden, she became conscious of her hand being intertwined with Ben's. She blushed and began to apologize, attempting to pull her hand away.

Ben clung to Shaya's hand for a moment. "Don't apologize," he said. "It feels nice."

Shaya's knees started to wobble. "It does," she acknowledged. "But it's lunchtime." Shaya pulled her hand away and turned to Jexi. "Congrats!" she said. "Let's find some food."

Jexi nodded. "Yeah, I'm hungry too. Winning creates such an appetite!"

Hunter gathered the golf balls. "I'll take the balls and clubs back to the office," he said. "Ben, will you give me a hand?"

"Sure," Ben replied. "See you, girls, later."

"Are we meeting at the bottom of the sparkly staircase?" Jexi asked.

"Yes," said Hunter. "Let's meet at six. That will give us a bit of time to talk before we go to our tables."

Shaya grabbed Jexi's arm and began pulling her off the course. "Sounds good!" she hollered back to the guys as they walked away.

As the girls walked to the cafe for lunch, Jexi asked Shaya, "What was the big hurry to get out of there?"

"No rush. I'm just really hungry," Shaya lied. She knew that didn't sound convincing and that Jexi wouldn't buy it for a second. But she was hoping that Jexi would let it drop so she didn't have to talk about it. She was nervous enough about the formal night later and she just wanted some quiet time to think.

Jexi tossed a sly smile. "Say what you want, but I saw you two holding hands back there," she quipped.

Shaya said, "Yeah, yeah, yeah, I know. But can we just focus on lunch, please? I don't really want to discuss this right now. I promise we'll talk later, okay? You know I need to process first."

Jexi nodded her head. "Okay. I understand," she replied. "Let's get some lunch. We need to eat and then rest up for the formal night tonight!"

CHAPTER ELEVEN

After the girls finished eating lunch, they walked toward their cabin. Once they were at their cabin, Shaya looked at the list of amenities onboard.

"Let's get a massage this afternoon," Shaya said. "They have a spa here! It would be so posh to pamper ourselves!"

Jexi had sprawled herself on her bed and was lying on her back. She had closed her eyes and was rubbing her head. "A massage does sound nice," she responded. "I'm pretty tense."

Shaya picked up the cabin phone and called the spa number. Jexi could hear her talking with the receptionist. "Hi, I'd like to book two massages for me and my friend, please." There was a slight pause. "Three o'clock? Yes, that will be perfect." Jexi heard another pause. "Shaya and Jexi, J-E-X-I," she spelled. "Yes, thank you. We'll see you then." Shaya hung up the phone. "We have massages reserved for three o'clock," she said.

Jexi opened her eyes. "I am looking forward to it," she said. "But if we stay in the room until then, I'm going to fall asleep. What else is there to do while we wait?"

Shaya looked at the list of open events. "There is bingo or adult coloring. What do you think of one of those?"

Jexi replied, "You know, I haven't colored in years. I used to enjoy it so much. Let's go there. Besides, we have already played bingo."

Shaya agreed. "I haven't colored in a long time either. I hope I remember how to stay in the lines. Are you ready?"

The girls made their way to the room where the coloring was being held. Jexi was surprised to see the number of options they had available to color. There were pictures of animals, mandalas, fairies, nature scenes, and abstract designs.

Jexi picked out a mandala to color and Shaya picked out an abstract image. They found a table and sat down. There were several different mediums in which to color, crayons, colored pencils, markers, pastels, and even watercolors. Jexi and Shaya both selected to use colored pencils and spent some time coloring their pictures. One of them would say something every so often, but much of their time was spent in companionable silence.

After about an hour, both girls had finished their pictures. "That was so oddly satisfying," Shaya commented. "I had a good time."

"Yeah, that was nice," Jexi added. "It took me back to my childhood!"

They walked back to their cabin to put their pictures in their suitcases.

"It's almost two-thirty," Jexi mentioned. "Should we start heading toward the spa?"

"Yep," Shaya said. "Hey Jex, I'm nervous about tonight."

"Nervous about seeing Ben?" Jexi asked. "You've been hanging out with him for a few days now. Why would tonight be different?"

Shaya took a moment to respond, "It's hard to explain. I feel drawn to him, and I know he is going to look so yummy in his tux. It is going to be more difficult to keep my walls up."

"Okay, um, go with me on this," Jexi answered. "Why, pray tell, would you want to keep your walls up with him after you've had these great days together? Why not just give in to the feeling?"

"I have to consider what is going to happen with us beyond this week. After tomorrow, we will be going our separate ways, and I am not interested in a long-distance relationship. We tried that and failed. I don't want to be hurt like that again," Shaya explained.

Jexi's expression turned to one of understanding. "I see," she said. "That makes sense. I'm sorry I pushed."

"I know I am acting strange, Jex. Thank you for being patient with me," Shaya said. "I have never loved anyone other than Ben. Running into him and spending time with him has stirred up a lot of feelings I wasn't prepared to face this week."

"I bet," Jexi replied. "Well, let's go get massaged. That will help us both to feel better."

Shaya smiled. "Yeah, no doubt!"

The girls walked to the spa and checked in at the reception desk. Two massage therapists came to the entrance and called them back. They walked down a dimly lit hallway and into an open area with several rooms around the perimeter of the rectangular space. "My name is Molly," the first therapist said to Jexi. "We'll be in room five."

The other woman looked at Shaya, "I'm Kaytlin, and we'll be in room four. Do either of you need to use the restroom before we begin? If so, it's right at the end of the hall."

Jexi spoke up, "I'd like to use the restroom before we start," she said.

"No problem," said Molly. "Just come to room five when you're done. I'll be ready for you."

After the hour was up, the girls met in the lobby. "What did you think?" Shaya asked.

"Oh, my goodness! I am so relaxed, and my body feels like melted butter!" Jexi replied.

"If your hair is any indication, it looks like you got a good work over," Shaya said with a laugh.

Jexi attempted to smooth her hair down with a laugh, "That bad, huh?" she asked.

"Yes," Shaya answered. "Mine is the same way. We need to get back to the cabin to shower."

"And get ready for tonight," Jexi added. She saw Shaya roll her eyes. "You roll your eyes at me a lot."

"I know," Shaya answered. "That's because you say a lot of annoying things."

"Whatever," Jexi said as she rolled her eyes back at Shaya. "There. Now come on."

The two made their way back to their cabin and Jexi yelled, "Dibs on the shower!"

"Fine," Shaya said. "Go ahead."

Jexi showered and then exited the bathroom in her bathrobe. "All yours," she told Shaya.

Shaya jumped up and went into the bathroom to shower. While Shaya was in the bathroom, Jexi styled her hair and put on her makeup. She also put on her formal gown, which was a gown she had chosen specifically for this night. She hadn't let Brennan see it because she had wanted to surprise him. Her dress was deep purple and sleeveless. The bodice was beaded with rhinestones and the rhinestones cascaded down the skirt. The skirt of the dress was pleated asymmetrical tulle with a ribbon hem. The skirt was higher in the front than in the back and Jexi felt like a queen while she was wearing it. As she slid it on, she felt a bit of sadness again at this whole situation. She wouldn't let herself cry this time though; she didn't want to ruin her makeup.

Shaya got out of the shower and used the bathroom mirror to primp for the evening. She wanted to look amazing, so she took her time with her makeup. She chose smoky eyes and a subtle lip color that wouldn't be too overwhelming. She chose to leave her hair down and only pull the sides back away from her face. Not that she was trying to please Ben, but she remembered how much he liked her hair this way. She added a sparkly silver hair clip to complete the look. She gazed at her reflection in the mirror and decided she looked pretty darn good. She stepped out of the bathroom and saw Jexi in her dress. "WOW! You look spectacular!" she exclaimed.

"Thank you. So do you . . . almost." Jexi replied. "You need to get your dress on because we are running out of time."

Shaya reached into the closet and pulled out her dress. As she unzipped the bag, she noticed Jexi was watching her. "I'll get dressed in the bathroom," Shaya told Jexi. She took the bag into the bathroom and stepped into her dress. The very dress that she wore on Jexi's wedding day. The dress that was supposed to have been her bridesmaid dress. "I hope you will be okay with this, Jex." She whispered to herself.

When Shaya stepped out of the bathroom, she heard Jexi let out a small gasp. "Jex?" she asked. "You okay?"

Jexi had her hand over her mouth, and she lowered it to her side. "Yeah, I'm fine. I knew you were going to have to wear that dress, but I didn't think it would bother me that much." She felt her stomach lurch. "I thought it was getting better, you know?"

Shaya stood next to her and sighed. "Yeah, I know. I'm sorry."

Jexi looked at her. "It's not your fault," she said. "You don't need to say you're sorry. It's Brennan who needs to apologize."

"But I'm sorry I didn't have time to find another dress for the trip. I know this is hard for you," Shaya said softly.

"That wasn't your fault either," Jexi replied. "Shaya, I promise I'm not upset with you!" Tears started to fill Jexi's eyes. "I just, I just, didn't expect to feel this way." She sniffed and attempted to keep the tears from falling. "Um, I'm not so sure about this after all."

Shaya looked puzzled. "Not sure about what?" she asked.

"Tonight. This formal night," Jexi responded. "I don't think I want to go. I mean, seeing you in the dress, all the sadness that I'm feeling, I really don't want to be a downer on what is supposed to be a fun evening."

Shaya pulled Jexi into a hug. "Are you sure? You look AHHHHH-mazing. It would be a shame to not let everyone see you," she said, in an attempt to lighten the mood.

"Yeah, I'm sure," Jexi answered. "Thanks, but I really think I'd like to take a walk by myself. Maybe after a bit and if I've cleared my head, I can join you then."

"Alright. I will save your seat," Shaya said. "But if I don't get out of here, I'll be late meeting the guys. Plus, I might also start crying with you."

"I'll walk with you part of the way," Jexi said.

The girls walked out of the cabin and toward the massive glitter staircase. Shortly before they reached it, Jexi turned to go toward the deck. "Here is where I take my leave," she said. "Tell the guys I'm sorry for not coming."

Shaya looked at her friend. "Okay, I'll tell them," she said, and started walking away. She paused and reached back for Jexi's hand. "Jex, you're not alone." Shaya released her hand and continued down the stairs. She couldn't help but whisper a short prayer for Jexi as she walked. "Lord, cover Jexi with Your presence and Your love. Show her she isn't alone and that You are always with her."

Jexi headed for the deck. She knew it wouldn't be crowded because almost everyone would be at dinner. She noticed that the sun was setting, and the sight was spectacular over the water. Brennan should be here, she thought. What happened? They had been so happy. She wanted it to all make sense, but there was no clarity for her when it came to that subject. She continued walking along the deck. With each step, she could feel herself become more and more angry. Her neck heated and she could feel her cheeks burn. How dare he?! she screamed in her head. How dare he do this to me? I didn't do anything wrong! I would have been an amazing wife to him! All of a sudden, he decided he wasn't in love anymore? Oh, I am so furious! Then she felt the tears. They were warm on her cheeks and there were several of them. This time she didn't try to stop them. This time she let them flow. She stopped toward the back of the deck where she stood the first night on the ship. This time she just cried.

After a few minutes of crying, Jexi wiped her tears with a tissue. She knew she had ruined her makeup, but since she wasn't planning on going to dinner, she didn't really care. Suddenly she noticed a warm breeze blowing across her face and a stirring in her heart. This felt familiar and as the breeze died down, she started to think about the things Shaya had told her.

Shaya had told her that she wasn't alone. Jexi thought that she was saying that Shaya would always be by her side, but now she was starting to wonder if she meant something a little different. She thought, Is Shaya talking about God? Could He be here? Right here? With me? God? Is that You? Immediately the warm breeze returned and seemed to blow right through her heart, leaving a sense of warmth and serenity.

Shaya cascaded down the stairs where the guys were waiting. Ben's eyes lit up when he saw her. The look on his face made her feel beautiful and loved. When she reached the bottom, she smiled and said, "Hi, guys. I hope I'm not late."

Ben didn't say anything, he just stared at her. Hunter laughed, "Evidently, he is speechless. You aren't late. Where is Jexi?"

"She may join us later," Shaya replied. She thought she noticed a slight look of disappointment on Hunter's face. "She's having a rough evening."

Shaya and the guys headed toward the dining room. The photographer was standing outside the entrance snapping pictures as the guests entered. Ben took Shaya's hand and stepped into position for a photo. "What are we doing?" Shaya asked.

"We're getting a picture taken. What does it look like?" Ben replied with a wicked smile.

Shaya responded with a smile. She couldn't help but think of Jexi right then. What was she doing? I wish she was here to get our picture together. She added another short prayer. Lord, take care of my friend. Shaya felt a sense of warmth and knew God had responded with a yes.

Just before Shaya, Ben, and Hunter entered the dining room Hunter stopped. "Shaya, you can take my seat with Ben tonight. I'm going to look for Jexi if you don't mind."

Jexi continued staring out over the water as the ship moved along. Tomorrow would be their last day at sea. Then it would be time to go home. Home! Jexi thought. Where is home? She knew that the lease to the apartment was going to expire two days after her return. What was she going to do then? She was supposed to be living with Brennan. I guess I could go live with Mom and Dad, she mused. Then she shuddered. No, I don't want to do that, she realized. I don't think that would work out for any of us. I love them dearly, but that probably isn't the best idea. But where would she live? She didn't want to stay in the same apartment, but she hadn't had time to look for anything new. She could ask her brother and his wife if she could stay with them. But as soon as that thought entered her mind, she threw it out again. She didn't want to intrude on their life together. She started to worry. Was she going to be able to find a place to live within two days?

"There you are," Hunter said, interrupting her thoughts.

Jexi whirled around at the sound of the familiar voice. Oh, no! she thought. It's Hunter and I am a mess! She tried to smooth her face, but she already knew that her makeup was wrecked. It was as good as it was going to get. She stood up straight and waved at him. "Hi!" she said.

"I've been looking for you," Hunter stated.

"Me?" Jexi asked. "Why? Didn't Shaya tell you I wasn't coming to dinner? And aren't you missing your formal night?"

"Yes, she did," he replied. "And yes I am. But a bet is a bet and I want to pay up."

Jexi blinked her eyes. She had completely forgotten about the bet from earlier. "Oh, yeah," she answered. "You did lose."

Hunter reached into his breast pocket and pulled out a small box and handed it to Jexi. "Don't worry, it's not a key chain," he joked.

Jexi couldn't believe her eyes. The box was wrapped and looked very fancy. She stammered out a small laugh, "Um, yeah. But this looks like more than a silly trinket."

"Nobody said it needed to be a silly trinket. You said a souvenir. That's what I got you. A simple souvenir," Hunter said.

"But," objected Jexi, "it was supposed to be under ten dollars. This box alone looks like it cost ten dollars."

"Just open it, please," Hunter pleaded.

"Okay, okay," Jexi replied. She glanced at Hunter just before she opened the gift. Hunter's face looked excited. What is this guy up to? she wondered.

She tore off the wrapping paper to find a flat, blue-colored box. She opened the box and gasped loudly. "Hunter!" she exclaimed. "What did you do? This, this, this is way too much!" She pulled out a dainty sterling silver bracelet with amethyst teardrop links. Each link was separated with small silver circular links. It was breathtaking.

"Nah, it's not too much," Hunter answered. "You've had a rough go of things lately. I saw this and I thought of you. Hopefully, you can cry some happy tears soon.

Jexi began to cry again. "I don't know what to say," she whispered. "This is so kind of you, but I am stunned. I mean, it was only supposed to be a . . . ."

Hunter cut her off. "You don't get to put parameters on what I deem is a perfectly acceptable gift. I'd like to think that we've become friends over the last several days and that is what this is. A gift from one friend to another."

"Friends, yes. But you barely know me." Jexi protested.

"I want you to look at this souvenir and remember that God loves you. You are a child of God which makes you royalty. Purple is the color of royalty. Plus, I know it's your favorite color." Hunter explained.

Jexi inwardly groaned. This moment had been almost perfect. "Well, thank you," she said to Hunter. "It is absolutely beautiful. I appreciate the gift."

"Here, let me help you put it on," Hunter said. "It will look fantastic on you! And it will match your dress!"

Jexi extended her arm and Hunter gently clasped the bracelet onto her wrist. His fingers brushed her wrist as he did so, and she shuddered with a feeling she'd never felt before. She looked up into his eyes and saw him looking back at her.

She cleared her throat and pulled back, admiring the bracelet. "It really is gorgeous," she said. "Thank you."

"You're welcome," Hunter replied. "How about we go get some grub?"

Jexi agreed and Hunter moved next to her and offered her his elbow. She slipped her hand in and allowed him to escort her to the dining hall, messy makeup and all.

CHAPTER TWELVE

The next day, Jexi woke up late in the morning. She had slept well and had enjoyed sleeping in. She sat up, yawned, and stretched. As she did, she saw Shaya sitting at the desk, reading her Bible. She admired Shaya's faith. Jexi wondered if there was any chance that she could believe as Shaya did. She had started to feel something different that she couldn't explain but she wasn't convinced that was anything more than her imagination.

Shaya looked up from her reading. "Good morning, Sleepy Head. Did you sleep well?" she asked.

"Yes," Jexi replied. "One of the best night's sleeps I've had since . . . well, you know. I'm sorry I slept past breakfast."

Shaya smiled. "No worries. I had an early breakfast with Ben."

Jexi looked down at her hands and asked, "Can I talk to you about something?"

"Duh!" Shaya responded. "I'm your best friend. You can talk to me about anything!" She closed her Bible and placed it on the bed beside her. She leaned forward to indicate that she was ready to give Jexi her full attention.

"Well, something weird happened last night." Jexi stopped and took a breath. "You know the bet Hunter and I made at mini golf, right?"

Shaya nodded. "Yes."

Jexi continued. "Well, he gave me the souvenir I earned by whooping him."

Shaya giggled. "You sure showed him!"

Jexi smiled. "I did, didn't I? But anyway, this is what he gave me." She held out her arm to show Shaya the bracelet.

Shaya gasped in shock and her eyes went wide. "Are you kidding me? That is gorgeous. And EXPENSIVE!"

"I know, right?!" Jexi answered. "Much more than the ten-dollar limit that we agreed on. But what's bothering me is more about what he said than what he gave me." She paused before continuing. "He said that I am a child of God and that means I am royalty. He said that purple is the color of royalty. I have heard before that I am a child of God, but what does that mean, that I am considered royalty?"

Shaya reached for her Bible again. "Let me read a verse that explains what he's talking about." She looked at the index in the back and found what she was looking for. "Okay, Galatians chapter four, verses six and seven." She flipped through some pages and found the book of Galatians. "And because we are His children, God has sent the Spirit of His Son into our hearts, prompting us to call out, 'Abba, Father.' Now you are no longer a slave but God's own child. And since you are His child, God has made you His heir."

Jexi paused for a moment in thought. Then she began to speak. "So, because I am a child of God, I am also an heir of God? An heir to what, though?"

"The kingdom of God," Shaya replied. "God is the King of all kings and His kingdom is also ours simply for being His child."

Jexi's brow furrowed. "I hadn't even thought of it that way," she stated. I don't understand all this God and Jesus stuff."

Shaya turned to another book in her Bible. "Let me read first Peter chapter two, verse nine." She flipped a few more pages. "But you are a chosen people, a royal priesthood, a holy nation, God's special possession, that you may declare the praises of Him who called you out of darkness into His wonderful light."

Jexi responded, "It sort of makes a little sense. But I'm still not sure how that makes me royalty. But thanks for helping, Shaya. I do love purple, though."

Shaya laughed. "Yes, you do. And if I'm honest, Hunter picked out the perfect gift for you. It's really nice."

Jexi shifted uncomfortably.

"Are you starting to have feelings for him?" Shaya asked.

Jexi sat straight up. "No way!" she answered. "He's really nice, but no, no, no. I'm not over Brennan yet! Remember, I was supposed to be married and on my honeymoon trip."

Shaya looked at her friend. "Yes, I know. But there is a different look in your eyes when Hunter is around. I needed to ask."

Jexi threw a pillow at her friend, hitting her in the face. "Don't be ridiculous! Anyway, tell me about last night with Ben. Oh . . . AND breakfast!"

Shaya blushed. "Well, last night I ordered chicken, and he had a medium rare steak." She paused. "This morning, we both had omelets. He put hot peppers in his. I put mushrooms in mine."

Jexi looked at her sideways. "That's not what I meant, and you know it," she said with feigned annoyance.

Shaya sighed. "Okay, okay! It's no big deal, really. And, nothing happened, if that's what you're wondering! We just had a nice time together, talking. We understand that after this cruise, we won't see each other again and I'm sure neither one of us wants to do the long-distance thing. That's it."

"So, it's over?" Jexi asked.

"Jex, it never really started to begin with. While it was super great to see him, I think we both knew that it wouldn't work. So, we just spent a few nice days together," Shaya said sadly.

"I'm sorry that it ended up like this," Jexi said.

Shaya looked up and said, "Let's not make a big issue of this. Let's just go spend one last day with the guys and have fun."

Jexi nodded. "That's a great idea!"

The girls got dressed and prepped for the day. It was their last day on the ship, and they were going to just wander around and have fun. Before they left their cabin, Shaya sent a quick text to Ben to let him know they were on their way. They grabbed their room keys and headed out to meet the guys. Jexi wanted another picture on the glittering staircase so that is where they decided to meet up to start the day.

The girls took a few silly pictures before Jexi requested, "Hey, Ben, come stand by Shaya so I can get a picture of the two of you."

Shaya jammed her elbow into Jexi's side. Jexi thought she was surely in deep trouble but when she looked at Shaya, she was grinning. "That's fine, but you and Hunter are next," she announced.

Jexi blushed but went to stand by Hunter. He put his arm around her shoulders, and they smiled for the picture.

Just then, a cute elderly couple passed by. "Would you like me to take a picture of all of you together?" the blue-haired lady asked.

Hunter responded, "Yes, that would be great!"

The lady took Shaya's phone and took several pictures of the four of them. "All done!" she announced, and she returned Shaya's phone to her. "You all look so happy together! You are blessed."

"Oh, we aren't . . ." Jexi started to say.

Hunter quickly interrupted. "Thank you for your kindness. Have a blessed day."

After they took pictures, the group walked to the top deck to play shuffleboard. Ben was proud of himself for winning the game. He jumped up and down and hugged Shaya. As much as she enjoyed the hug, she knew she had to pull away. Once again, Ben looked hurt by her resistance, but he didn't say anything about it.

Jexi noticed Shaya pull back from Ben and felt sad for her. It's too bad they won't see each other after this, she thought. Ben would make her so happy.

After shuffleboard, they went to the pizza place to get lunch. While they ate, they laughed and had fun just being together. When they had finished their meal, they went to the Photomat to get their pictures developed. They were all glad to have visible memories of the trip.

"You know, we could save a lot of money if we developed these on land," Shaya said.

"Sure," Jexi replied. "But we live in different cities, which would make that rather difficult."

Ben smiled. "We could always come to Kansas City to pick them up." He tossed a sly smile to Shaya.

That afternoon, the group went to the pool to swim and lounge. When they saw the crowded pool, they hesitated.

"Nope," Shaya said. "Way too many people." She started to walk away.

"Wait, Shaya," Ben called. "There are some chairs over here away from the pool. How about we sit over there?"

"Oh, alright," Shaya agreed. "But I am not going swimming. There is literally no space in that pool!"

As they settled into the chairs, Hunter pulled over a small table. "I've got a deck of cards that I picked up at the gift shop," he said. "Let's play a game."

"What game?" Jexi asked.

"How about rummy?" Ben proposed. "If my memory is correct, one of us is an expert rummy player." He looked at Shaya and winked.

Shaya smiled sheepishly and started to respond, but Hunter beat her to it. "Dude, you don't need to brag like that."

"Whatever!" Ben replied. "I'm talking about Shaya, not me!"

Jexi was a little surprised. She was learning so much about her best friend on this trip. She couldn't help but be a little jealous that Ben seemed to know things about Shaya that she didn't know until now. She wondered why Shaya had kept some of these hidden from her. It stung.

Hunter shuffled the cards and dealt. After five hands of rummy, Shaya had won all but one.

"Listen, bestie," Jexi said to Shaya. "I can't believe you have kept that little gem of a skill such a secret. You are GOOD!"

Ben looked at his watch. It was getting close to dinnertime. "I'm hungry," he stated.

"Me too," said Jexi. "Where should we eat tonight?"

Shaya giggled. "We have so many options! There is no way anyone can visit each restaurant on this ship in one week!" "What about the buffet?" suggested Jexi. "We haven't been able to have dinner there, yet."

Hunter nodded. "Yes," he agreed, "Let's do that!"

The group gathered their things and headed toward the buffet room for their final dinner. Shaya felt sadness welling up inside her. She never expected to see Ben again, yet here she was, preparing to say goodbye to the love of her life. She choked back tears that threatened to fall. Not tonight, she thought. I'll save that for another day. She felt Ben's hand reach for hers but this time she didn't pull away. For the moment, she felt warm and safe.

They entered the enormous room, with only a small crowd. Once again, Jexi was amazed at the amount of food available. There were several types of soups, sushi, grilled tomatoes, mozzarella sticks, and even chicken nuggets! There were numerous salads. They had pasta, fish, chicken, duck, lobster, turkey, and beef.

On a separate wall were the desserts. Desserts Jexi had never even heard of were laid out. She had no idea what a mocha crème brûlée was, but it sure sounded good! There were apple pie, chocolate mousse, chocolate cake, and several flavors of cheesecake.

They jumped in line and filled their plates. They didn't talk a lot through dinner. It seemed that the sadness of knowing that this was their last night together rested heavily on all of them.

"Dinner was delicious," Shaya commented, as she leaned back and patted her stomach. "I won't need to eat for the next three days!"

"Yes, it certainly was," Hunter responded in agreement.

Jexi nodded. "I'm stuffed."

"Hey, Jexi, we need to get back to the cabin to pack," Shaya pointed out.

Jexi looked at her. "Yeah, we also need to get to bed before we normally do. We have to disembark really early in the morning."

Ben looked at Hunter and then at Jexi. "Would you guys mind if Shaya and I took a short walk before you do all that?" he asked.

Shaya's heart froze. What could he possibly want? she thought. She stuttered, "We really need to be packing though."

"It will be a short walk, I promise." Ben replied.

"Of course, we don't mind," Jexi interjected, garnering a fearful look from Shaya. "I'll help by getting your packing started for you. Hunter, do you mind walking me to my room? There may be creeps lurking in the hallways."

Shaya stammered, "Oh, well then, I guess we can go, Ben. Um, thanks, Jexi."

Hunter stood up and motioned to Jexi. "I will be happy to escort you, m'lady!" Hunter and Jexi started walking in the direction of the girls' cabin.

Ben looked at Shaya, "I didn't mean to catch you off guard. We can talk right here if you'd prefer."

"No, it's okay. I would like to walk. It's a beautiful night." Shaya responded. The two stood up from the table and Ben reached for Shaya's hand. "Ben, what are you doing? You know this can't happen." Shaya stated.

Ben did not relent, he continued to hold out his hand for hers. "Shay, please."

Shaya surrendered and placed her hand in Ben's. They walked out of the buffet and toward the elevator. "What's this about, Ben?" Shaya asked.

Ben didn't respond until they were on the elevator. He turned to face Shaya and she could see the desperation in his eyes. "Shaya, I don't want to lose you again. These past few days have been amazing. Tomorrow, we go back to our lives with nothing but memories and a few pictures." He paused and took a breath. "Shay—"

Just then, the elevator door opened. Shaya and Ben stood in stunned silence. A voice from the corridor asked, "Are you going up or down?"

Ben turned to the man at the door, "Sorry. We are actually getting off here."

Shaya followed Ben off the elevator, his words spinning in her mind like a pinwheel on a windy day.

Ben led Shaya to the railing, overlooking the vast ocean. "Shay," he continued, "please tell me you feel the same way. Please tell me you don't want to go back to last week . . . to life without me."

Shaya was dumbfounded. Yes, she knew now that she still loved him, but the reality of their situation was looming. "Ben, I don't know what to say. We live hundreds of miles apart." She pointed to the dark water. "There may as well be an ocean between us."

Ben took her hands in his, "It's not THAT far. Besides, I think you are worth fighting for, distance or not."

Shaya felt tears rolling down her cheeks. She had waited her whole adult life to hear someone say those words to her. "Ben—"

Ben cut off her words with a gentle kiss. "You don't have to answer me now. But I'm not finished with this conversation," he whispered to her.

Ben led her back to the elevator, "I promised it would be a quick walk. Let's get you back to pack," he said.

Meanwhile, Hunter and Jexi barely spoke for a while as they walked. Hunter broke the silence by asking Jexi a question. "Have you had a good time on this cruise?"

"Yes," Jexi answered. "A lot more fun than I thought I would have, to be honest. I really expected to spend the whole cruise crying in our cabin."

"I'm sorry for what happened to you," Hunter said softly. "No self-respecting man would ever do that to a lady."

"Thanks," Jexi said, "But it isn't your fault. I don't know why Brennan didn't talk about it with me before the wedding. I wish he would have. If he had, then I don't think him standing me up would have been as much of a shock." She turned to Hunter. "Have you ever been married?" she asked.

"No," Hunter replied. "I haven't even dated anyone that I have considered marrying. I guess I just haven't found the right one."

"She's out there," Jexi said encouragingly. "Don't give up."

Hunter looked at Jexi. He truly felt that their meeting was not a coincidence and that God had something in the works. He just wasn't sure what that might be. "Well," he said, "as my mom always tells me, I have plenty of time to find a wife."

Jexi laughed. "Your mom is very wise," she said. "You should listen to her."

"She would love you for saying that," Hunter said. "Too bad we won't see each other again. I've really had fun with you."

They approached the door of the cabin and stopped. Jexi pulled out her key and unlocked the door. She turned to look at Hunter. "I've had fun with you too," she said. "I'm sorry that you took such a beating at mini golf, but I did warn you."

Hunter grinned. "That's okay," he said. "It gave me the opportunity to give you something special." He reached out to hug her.

Jexi responded by hugging him back. She was surprised at how comforting his embrace was. As Hunter's arms enveloped her, Jexi felt the same feeling that she had when he had put her bracelet on her wrist. She also felt her knees get somewhat weak. She briefly noted that Brennan never made her feel this way. *What is happening?* she thought. *Shaya can't be right. I don't have feelings for this guy! I'm still in love with Brennan.* She quickly stepped back out of the hug. It seemed as if Hunter didn't want to let her go, but he respected her body language and dropped his arms to his side.

"Thank you for walking me back," Jexi said. "I am going to get started on that packing. We will meet you and Ben at the gate in the morning to say goodbye, right?"

"Right," Hunter answered. "To say goodbye." Jexi thought she noted a hint of sadness in his voice.

"Goodnight," she said as she slipped into her cabin.

CHAPTER THIRTEEN

The next morning, the alarm clock sounded at six o'clock. Jexi groaned as she rolled over and smacked the clock to shut it off. "UGH!" she grunted.

Shaya laughed. "Come on, lazy. Time to get up."

"But it's so early!" Jexi argued.

Shaya threw her pillow at Jexi. "You can sleep when we get home. We have to get up and disembark. You can't live on this ship."

"Hey!" Jexi exclaimed. "That's not a bad idea! I can learn to shape towels into different animals."

"You, crazy nut," Shaya responded. "You can't do that and you know it. Get up already."

Shaya headed to the bathroom to brush her teeth and shower. Jexi told her, "Just wake me up when you're done in the bathroom."

Shaya rolled her eyes as she walked into the bathroom and shut the door. She was relieved that Jexi hadn't brought up last night's conversation with Ben. She wasn't ready to talk about that just yet. When Shaya was done getting ready, she hollered at Jexi. "Hey, get up! I'm done."

Jexi sat up and rubbed her eyes. "Okay, okay. I'm coming."

Jexi quickly got ready for the day and packed the last of her essentials. "Alright, I'm ready."

Shaya handed Jexi a glazed doughnut. "I grabbed these yesterday because I knew we wouldn't have time for breakfast," she said with a snicker.

"That is so like you to do that," Jexi said, giggling. She took the doughnut and ate it while Shaya ate an apple fritter.

The two were ready to go. Shaya called the front desk to have a bellhop come to help with their luggage. When he arrived, they led the way to the gate.

Shaya's heart was leaping in circles in her chest. She knew she would see Ben this morning and she knew he was expecting some sort of response. She had left him hanging, but honestly, she wasn't prepared to answer him. This was all too much for her and she needed ample time to process her feelings. Would he understand that? I guess I'll find out soon enough, she thought.

"SHAYA!" Jexi said loudly.

"What?" Shaya asked.

"I asked you a question and you are off in la-la land. What's up?" Jexi said.

"Oh, sorry," Shaya apologized. "What were you asking?"

"Do you want to take a bus or a taxi to the airport?" Jexi asked.

"A taxi would be less crowded. It will cost more, but I am not up for being crammed into a tiny bus seat, surrounded by strangers." Shaya responded.

"Okay. I'll get one when we get out there," Jexi replied. She spotted Hunter and Ben walking toward them. "Oh, look!" she announced. "There are Hunter and Ben! I wonder if they will take a taxi to the airport too! Maybe we can share a ride."

Shaya glanced at Jexi with a sideways glare. Why is she always doing this? she thought.

"Don't look at me like that. This is what you get for not telling me what you and Ben talked about last night!" Jexi said with a sly grin. "Did you honestly think I would just let this go?"

"No, you are like a dog with a bone. Why must you cause trouble?" Shaya asked.

"Grr, grr," Jexi growled jokingly. "I'm not trying to cause trouble. I simply want to know what is happening between you and Ben."

"You know I am going to tell you everything. I just need my processing time. Be patient, little puppy." Shaya teased.

"Okay, okay, I'll stop barking at you," Jexi said. Just at that moment, the boys walked up to them.

"Hey, girls!" Hunter said. "Ready to get back home?"

"NO!" the girls both said in unison.

Hunter and Ben laughed. "This has been really nice," said Ben.

"Well," said Shaya, "I guess it's time for us to walk down the ramp. They are going to kick us off in about twenty minutes anyhow."

"Are you two flying back?" asked Hunter.

Jexi responded, "Yes, we are. We are going to get a cab to the airport. What about you guys?"

Ben said, "Yes, we will be taking a flight back to Joplin, and then driving home to Baxter Springs."

Jexi looked at Shaya. "We could share the cab to the airport then. What do y'all think?"

"Shaya, is that okay with you?" Ben asked.

"The more, the merrier!" Shaya responded. "Lead the way."

Jexi hailed a cab and the four showed the bellhops which luggage was theirs to put into the trunk. Then they all climbed into the taxi.

The drive to the airport was quiet but tense. Each of them wanted to say something, but each of them hesitated. Once they reached the airport, they all breathed a collective sigh of relief.

As they walked to the terminals, Ben leaned close to Shaya and whispered, "I was serious about what I said last night. This conversation isn't over. I am going to call you as soon as I get home."

Shaya spun around to face him. She slowly dropped her bags and enveloped him in a hug. "I know. We will talk," she said into his neck. "I miss you already."

Ben placed a kiss on her forehead and responded, "Me too. More than I ever thought possible."

Shaya pushed him away, "Don't make this weird," she teased.

Hunter looked at Jexi and debated whether or not to hug her. Jexi looked just as uncomfortable.

"I hope that you have a nice and safe flight," Hunter said. "If you ever get bored, you've got my number."

"Yep, I sure do!" Jexi responded. "And likewise, if you get bored, you've got mine. I hope your flight is smooth as well."

Hunter decided to give her a goodbye hug and Jexi once again seemed to melt into his arms. She did not let the hug last very long though, and quickly picked up her carry-on bag. She looked at Shaya and Ben and thought about how good they looked together. She watched as Shaya stepped away from Ben's embrace.

"Are you ready, Shaya?" Jexi asked.

"I think so," Shaya responded with tears welling up in her eyes.

They all said their final goodbyes, and each walked to their designated gate. Jexi and Shaya said nothing as they walked to the gate and sat in the chairs.

The wait to board the plane seemed to last an eternity. Shaya reached into her purse and pulled out the picture of her and Ben. The tears that had welled up in her eyes began to fall, despite her best efforts to hold them back.

Jexi reached over and put her arm around Shaya. "You still love him."

Shaya sniffled and nodded. "Yeah, I do. Dang it!"

Jexi searched her brain for something wise to say. "Well," she began, "you always say there are no coincidences. Was this a divine plan? Maybe God will work it to bring the two of you back together?"

Shaya slowly turned her head toward Jexi. "Seriously? Now you believe in a divine plan?" she asked, with a teary laugh.

Jexi attempted to defend herself. 'Um, I'm just trying to help. You're the one who said that, not me."

Just then, the flight attendant called their flight to Kansas City. They quietly boarded the plane and took their seats.

"By the way," Jexi said, "I just remembered I am homeless. My lease expires in two days."

"Is that a hint?" Shaya asked accusingly.

"Yeah, sort of," Jexi answered. "Plus, it's a good segue to change the subject. What am I going to do?"

"You could renew your lease," Shaya said.

"No, I can't," Jexi said. "If I wanted to renew my lease, I would have had to let my landlord know thirty days ago. But the worst part about it is that Brennan and I canceled the lease, so it's not renewable. As a matter of fact, I don't even know where my things are right now. What a pickle!"

"Oh, you and your pickles!" exclaimed Shaya. "How many of your pickles have I saved you from already?"

"TWO! Exactly two." Jexi protested.

"Is that all?" Shaya asked. "Hmm. Seems like there were more. Oh, well."

Jexi gave her a sour look. "Thanks a lot, bestie."

"Look, we can call your parents to see if they know where your things are," Shaya stated. "Then we can start looking for a place for you. It might be hard, getting a place within two days." The two sat in silence for a few minutes. "You can stay with me," Shaya said. "I can clean out my home office and turn it back into a bedroom."

"You would do that for me?" Jexi asked. "Even though you think I'm annoying?"

"It's just so I can add another pickle save to the list." Shaya teased. "I'm serious, though. You are my best friend, and I don't want you to be homeless under the I-70 Bridge."

"So, all you want are bragging rights," Jexi mumbled. "But it's not like I have a lot of other options. So, I'll take it! Thanks!"

"Of course, you'll take it," Shaya said. "After all, I am the pickle rescuer."

Jexi rolled her eyes. "Maybe it would be better if I go to live with my parents."

"Too late! No takebacks!" Shaya said. "But don't be up in my grill all the time. You know I need my quiet space," she added with a laugh.

"Okay, okay," Jexi said. "Stop begging! I'll move in with you."

The flight went very smoothly, and the girls chatted the entire way home. When they arrived at the Kansas City Airport, Jexi's parents were there to pick them up.

Jexi's mom and dad both gave her a huge hug and were very excited to see her. Jexi's mom turned and hugged Shaya also. "We've missed you both!" she said.

"You look rested and happy," Jexi's dad said.

"We are rested and happy, Dad," replied Jexi. "The cruise was incredible. There is so much to share, but not right now. Let's get together for lunch on Sunday."

"Where are we taking you?" Jexi's mom asked.

"Shaya's apartment, please," answered Jexi. "I am going to be staying with her for a while."

Jexi's mom looked to be a little disappointed. "Oh, I thought you would come to stay with your dad and me," she said.

"Oh, Mom, that is so sweet of you," Jexi said. "But I think it will be better for me to stay with Shaya. I'll only be a few miles away. But do you happen to know where my things are from my apartment? The movers were supposed to pick everything up this week and deliver it to the new house."

Jexi's dad spoke up. "Yes, we do. We talked with Brennan while you were on the cruise and had the movers bring your things to our house. They are in your old bedroom. Brennan took most of the furniture."

Jexi scowled. "Of course he did," she murmured. "He stands me up on our wedding day and now he has the furniture we bought together. I'm going to give him a call and . . . ."

"But we got to go on the honeymoon and rack up his credit card with excursions," Shaya said with a laugh. "Look, Jex, it's just furniture. I have everything we need at my house. All you need to bring is a bed and your personal items. We will get you more furniture when you need it. You can sleep on the couch tonight and we'll pick up your bed tomorrow."

Jexi calmed down. "Yeah, you're right," she said. "Thanks."

The four of them piled into the car and drove to Shaya's apartment. Jexi's parents shared updates of their life over the past week, but they didn't push the girls to talk about their trip or their plans.

When they arrived at the apartment, Jexi hugged her parents and thanked them for picking them up at the airport. She promised to call the next day and assured them that she would be okay.

Jexi was exhausted as she hauled her luggage into Shaya's apartment. All she wanted to do was lay down and sleep for days. "Would you be open to a little nap time before we get back to reality?" Jexi asked.

Shaya released a big sigh, "I'm sure glad you mentioned that! I am worn out!" she replied. "Let me grab a blanket and pillow for you." She disappeared down the hallway and opened the closet door.

Jexi sat on the couch and rested her head on the headrest. She was asleep before Shay even returned.

CHAPTER FOURTEEN

At four o'clock, Jexi woke up and stretched. She rubbed her eyes and looked at her phone. She was surprised that she'd slept until four o'clock, but then again, she was so tired. She looked around and didn't see Shaya. She must still be asleep, she thought. But when she listened carefully, she could hear Shaya's voice in her bedroom. I wonder who she's talking to, she mused. Could it be Ben?

Shaya had been deep into a lovely dream when her phone rang. She had to volume down so it wouldn't disturb Jexi but it was loud enough to wake Shaya. She rolled over and looked at the display. Ben! He had kept his promise to call me when he got home, she thought excitedly. Should I answer it or play hard to get? Ahh, I might as well talk to him. She hit the talk button. "Hey, Ben," she said.

While Shaya talked on the phone, Jexi's stomach rumbled. She suddenly realized how hungry she was. The girls had snacked on the plane trip home but hadn't really had a solid meal all day. She pondered whether or not to bother Shaya while she was on the phone. But if it's Ben, she won't want me to interrupt, she deduced. I'm a grown woman, I can find some things to put together some sort of dinner.

Jexi stood up and ambled to the kitchen. She opened some cabinets and looked in the pantry. She looked inside the refrigerator. All she could find were Skillet Surprise boxed meals, canned soup, and expired milk. Too bad Shaya didn't have anything to make for a meal! Oh, well, we can always order pizza, she thought. We will have to get to the grocery store soon!

Shaya ended her call with Ben and wondered if Jexi was still asleep. However, she thought she heard movement in the kitchen. She gathered herself together and exited the bedroom. She saw Jexi rummaging through the cabinets. "Are you hungry?" she asked.

Jexi jumped and spun around. "Oh, geez!" she squealed. "You scared me! And yes, I am famished. We really haven't eaten much today."

"Me too! But you aren't going to find anything in there," Shaya said with a laugh.

"I can see that," Jexi responded. "I guess with us going on the cruise, you haven't really had a chance to get to the store."

"We left on grocery day," Shaya said.

"Well, we can order pizza," Jexi suggested. "Or we can get something delivered."

"I don't really want pizza," Shaya answered. "Why don't we walk down to the sandwich shop on the corner? They sell Pepsi there and I could use a boost of caffeine."

Jexi shut the last cabinet and agreed. "That sounds delicious."

The girls freshened up a little and then walked the short block and a half to the sandwich shop. When they walked in, there was only one other couple there eating. They approached the counter to place their orders.

Once they had received their food, they sat down at one of the tables and began eating. For a few minutes, there was silence because they both had their mouths filled with food. Jexi was the first to talk. "I am going to need to get a job soon. I am really scared that I won't be able to support myself."

"You are so forgetful. Didn't you support yourself before you met Brennan?" Shaya reminded. "I know he took care of you and was planning to let you stay home, but you are no stranger to working."

Jexi paused before she answered. "I know. I know. But it feels like it's been so long. What if I don't have the right skills anymore? What would I even do? I can't even remember how to interview correctly! And what will I do for a résumé?" Jexi felt herself begin to panic.

"Then you will learn new skills! And we can go over interview questions together. You don't have to face this scary world all on your own," Shaya replied. "Thankfully, I am an expert at writing résumés. We'll create one and start searching online as soon as we get your room ready. First things first."

"Thank you, Shay. I am blessed to have you as my best friend," Jexi said as she breathed a calming breath.

Shaya gave Jexi a sideways look. "Did you just say BLESSED?" she asked with a giggle. "You know where blessings come from, right?"

"Yeah, you've told me over and over that blessings come from God," Jexi replied. "But you know what I mean. I am just thankful for you, that's all. But we don't need to make a big deal about it."

"Okay, I won't," Shaya said and added under her breath, "Not today anyway."

"But I do have a lot that I need to figure out," Jexi stated. "I need a job, a place to live, furniture, stability—"

"Hold up! You don't have to figure it all out today." Shaya stated. "For the moment, you have a place to live and furniture. We can start with the job and stability."

"I guess you're right," Jexi conceded. "I just panicked about it all. It's so overwhelming. Especially trying to face reality without Brennan by my side. Everything is just so . . . just so . . . different."

"Do you even have an idea of what you'd like to do?" Shaya asked.

Jexi shook her head. "Nope! I know that I would like to help people in some way though."

"Thank goodness you didn't say you wanted to be a professional gamer!" Shaya said with a smile. "I would have had to kick you out before you even moved in!" She looked at Jexi's fake hurt face and added, "I'm just kidding. You can do whatever you want."

Jexi laughed. "Oh, no way!" she responded. "I may not know exactly what I want to do, but I don't think that is the path I want to travel."

Shaya looked at Jexi. "You don't want to hear this, but I have to say it. You need to pray about what job to take. God will direct you if you let Him."

Jexi sighed. "Okay, I hear what you're saying. And I will consider it, I promise. But on another note, I heard you talking on the phone this afternoon. You weren't by chance talking to Ben, were you?"

"Perhaps. Who wants to know?" Shaya retorted matter-of-factly.

"Curious minds," Jexi replied. "Plus, it gives me something to talk about other than my pathetic situation."

"Okay, yes, it was Ben. He is already talking about coming to visit. I'm not sure what to say to that," Shaya said.

"Wow! He must really want you back! He's still living in your hometown, right? Where was that again? Baxter Springs?" Jexi asked.

"Yeah, he is in Baxter Springs, Kansas. It isn't too far away for a vacation, but it is definitely far away for a relationship. It scares the figgle-snoots out of me." Shay replied.

"Figgle-snoots?!" Jexi looked at Shaya skeptically. "Are we just making up words now?"

"Isn't that what we do?" Shay asked with a giggle.

"Yeah, we do that a lot. So I'll allow it," Jexi said as she winked at Shaya. "Okay. You're terrified. I get it. But did you ever consider that maybe he's the ONE? Maybe he'll move up here. Or you could move back there! Y'all could get married in the church you grew up in, have beautiful babies, and live happily ever after!"

Shaya paused for a moment. "Of course, I have considered that he may be the ONE. He's the only man I have ever loved. I wanted to marry him. But he wasn't willing to leave Baxter Springs way back in the day, and I surely don't want to move back to Kansas. I wouldn't want to leave you. Plus, I have a great job and a decent life up here."

Jexi looked at Shaya with raised eyebrows. "Are you really that attached to Kansas City?" she asked cynically. "Besides, I know for a fact that Baxter Springs is only around three hours away. That really isn't that long of a drive to make a long-distance thing work."

Shaya considered the question. "Honestly, I don't know if I would say I'm attached. I'm comfortable. I have spent the last several years feeling like this is where I am supposed to be. However, Jex, you know I don't make any big decisions without prayer. I plan to take some time to ask for God's guidance. I promised I would follow where He leads me."

"And we all know how you are when you get into your comfort zones, that's for sure!" Jexi giggled. "Fine. If you pray first before making big decisions, then pray about this for sure! Ben is nuts about you and I know you want this! Plus, doesn't he deserve a second chance?"

Shaya took a long breath before she spoke. "Maybe. Here's the deal. I live my life, not by my will, but by God's will. If God's will is for me to give Ben a second chance, that's what I will do. That doesn't take away the fear, by any means, but it buys me some time." Shaya explained. She glanced at her watch. "Speaking of time, let's head home."

Jexi gathered their trash and took it to the trash can for disposal. Then she and Shaya walked back to the apartment, making small talk along the way.

The rest of the evening, the girls watched television and chatted. It had been a while since they had just hung out at home together, and it felt nice. At this moment, they had no worries or concerns about what the next day or their immediate futures held.

After a few hours, they both began to yawn. Even though they had napped earlier, the previous week had taken its toll and they were quite drowsy.

Shaya's phone chirped with a text, and she picked it up and read, "Miss you! Sleep well." She smiled. *Ben really is sweet. I could get* used to this attention, she thought. She typed a text back, "Goodnight . . . and I miss you too." Shaya hit send quickly before she changed her mind.

Jexi looked at her phone. Nothing. She was not sure if she was upset or happy about that. She wanted to have someone to talk to and love. She really wanted Brennan to change his mind. She wished she could call or text him. She looked at Shaya and thought about asking her if she thought it would be okay to text Brennan. She could see the smile on Shaya's face and decided not to bother her with it. She picked up her phone and quickly opened the texting app. It didn't take her long to find the thread with texts between her and Brennan and she typed out a short message. "We are home from the cruise. I miss you. Let's talk soon, okay?" Then before Shaya could see what she was doing, she closed the texting app. Somewhere in the back of her mind, she knew that if she didn't want Shaya to find out about this, then she probably shouldn't be reaching out to him, but she hadn't been able to help herself.

Shaya stood up and stretched. "I'm going to bed," she announced. "I've placed extra towels in the bathroom and there are blankets in the closet in case you get cold. If you need something else, wait until I wake up," she joked.

Jexi laughed. "I should be fine," she responded. "Thanks again, Shay."

"You're welcome," Shaya answered, and she walked toward her bedroom. "Good night, roomie."

"Good night," Jexi hollered after her. "Don't stay up all night talking to Ben!"

"Not tonight," Shaya replied. "I'm worn smooth. I'll be asleep before I finish my prayers."

After Shaya closed her bedroom door, Jexi looked at her phone. Still nothing. Why hasn't he responded? she thought. Doesn't he miss me? Maybe he's already in bed and just hasn't seen it yet. He'll respond in the morning. Having convinced herself of this, Jexi spread the sheets and blankets on the couch and then went to the bathroom to change and wash her face. By the time she returned to the living room, she was more than ready to get to sleep. She plopped down onto the sofa and was practically asleep before her head hit the pillow.

CHAPTER FIFTEEN

The next two weeks were filled with moving Jexi's furniture over to Shaya's place, filling the refrigerator and cabinets with food for two, filling out job applications, and getting used to being roommates. Jexi and Shaya were getting along quite well despite a few minor bumps in the road.

Shaya and Ben had been speaking every day, sometimes two or three times, since they returned home from the cruise. Jexi could see that things were moving quickly between them. Shaya had confessed that after praying a great deal about it, she had agreed to give Ben a second chance.

As the two women were on their nightly walk, out of nowhere, Shaya squealed, "Ben is going to be here tomorrow!"

Jexi giggled. "You are acting just like a girl in high school! But I do understand. I am really excited for you!"

Jexi's phone rang. She jumped and said with delight, "It must be Brennan!" She reached into her back pocket for her phone.

Shaya gave her a very quizzical look. "Brennan?" she asked disgustedly.

But Jexi had already started to answer the phone. She held her finger up to Shaya to signify that she needed a moment. She answered the phone, "Hello?"

Within a moment, Jexi's face fell, and the excitement left her voice. She listened to the person on the other end of the line for a bit. Then she replied. "Yes, I would like that. Thank you. I will see you Tuesday afternoon at one o'clock." Then she hung up the phone.

Shaya stared at her friend in disbelief. Brennan? she thought. Is she making plans to see Brennan on Tuesday?

Jexi looked at Shaya and knew immediately that she needed an explanation. She sighed. "It wasn't him," she said sadly. "But I have a job interview on Tuesday."

The look of disbelief remained with Shaya as she responded. "We will talk about the interview later. Why in the world would you be expecting Brennan to call you?!"

Jexi hung her head. "I may have texted him shortly after we got back home."

"What were you thinking?!" Shaya exploded. "The man walked out on you. No, actually, he never even showed up to walk out on you!"

"I know," Jexi answered. "I know that. But I just can't truly believe that he wanted to completely break it off with me. He just wasn't ready to get married is all. He still wants to be with me. All we need to do is get back together and allow time to heal our wounds. Then we'll get married when he's ready."

Shaya stopped walking and turned to Jexi. "Jexi, I know he turned your whole world upside down. But I want you to hear me and understand something. You deserve better than Brennan. You deserve someone who will cherish you, not hurt you. CLEARLY, he doesn't want to be with you. HE LEFT YOU AT THE CHURCH, IN YOUR WEDDING DRESS!"

Jexi stood still, as tears filled her eyes. "Shaya, I miss him so much my heart hurts. He was supposed to be my husband. I was prepared to spend the rest of my life with him. I can't give up."

Shaya looked at Jexi with compassion. "I know. And I know it hurts. But the more time you spend trying to win him back is less time you spend healing yourself. I've been holding back a little because I know how much your heart aches, but I have to say this. LET HIM GO. He isn't the one for you. I promise. I know that it is a terrible thing to hear, but you have to trust me!"

Jexi's shoulders slumped and she began to cry heavy tears. Shaya teared up as she pulled Jexi towards her and wrapped her arms around her. She whispered in Jexi's ear, but her words were not meant for Jexi. "Father God, You are the Almighty Healer. I'm asking You to rain down Your healing power on Jexi. Heal her heart and heal her mind. Help her see that she is loved by You and that's the only love she needs right now. Lord, wrap her in Your peace. In Jesus' name, I pray. Amen." Shaya released her grip and stepped back. She gave Jexi a reassuring smile.

Jexi stood up straight. She couldn't explain it, but she was feeling that peace again. It was almost as if the desire to cry had been extinguished and she was able to breathe calmly. She thought the peace that she had felt on the cruise was only because of the surroundings, but they were home now. Could that feeling have followed her home? She thought about the prayer that Shaya had said. *Could it be that the reason I'm feeling this peace is because of Shaya's prayer?*

Shaya noticed that Jexi had a puzzled look on her face. "Are you okay?" she asked her.

Jexi nodded and replied, "I think so. I am a little confused, though."

"About what?" Shaya inquired.

"Well," Jexi began to put her thoughts into words. "On the cruise, there were several moments where I felt calm and peaceful but couldn't explain it. I thought that it was just because the environment was so beautiful and serene. But I just experienced that same feeling here, right after you prayed. It was like a wave of tranquility surged through me. I just don't understand what that's all about."

Shaya grinned. She couldn't help it. She looked up towards Heaven and whispered a quiet, "Thank You, Lord!"

"What?" Jexi asked.

"Don't you remember when I told you about the peace of God while we were on the cruise?" Shaya responded. "I read that passage out of Philippians."

"Sort of," Jexi answered. "Can we look it up again when we get home?"

Shaya nearly did cartwheels out of excitement. "I can look it up right now on my phone!"

Shaya pulled out her phone and loaded the Bible app. She quickly looked up the verse. "Here it is! Philippians chapter four, verses six and seven." She began reading, "Do not be anxious about anything, but in every situation, by prayer and petition, with thanksgiving, present your requests to God. And the peace of God, which transcends all understanding, will guard your hearts and your minds in Christ Jesus." She lowered her phone and looked at Jexi. "That means that God can give us peace even when things here on earth are chaotic. THAT'S what you're feeling!"

Jexi tilted her head, "So, I just need to present my requests to God?" She got a little excited thinking about using this plan to get Brennan back.

Shaya groaned. "Really? Out of all this, that is the point you are focused on? Yes, we do present our requests to God. BUT what is more important is that we can have peace despite our situations because of God's love! God is not a vending machine, Jex. He loves us and wants what is best for us. A lot of times, what we think is best for us is actually what is the worst for us."

Jexi nodded her head and turned to walk toward home. Shaya followed. For the rest of the walk, the girls were silent. When they reached the apartment, Jexi disappeared into her bedroom. Shaya wanted to say more, but she could sense that Jexi was not ready to hear anymore. She walked into her own bedroom and dialed Ben's number.

CHAPTER SIXTEEN

The next morning was Saturday and Jexi awoke early. She knew that Ben would be arriving around noon, and she wanted to be at her parents' house and out of the way before he got to the apartment. Not that she didn't want to say hello, but honestly, she was a bit jealous of Shaya and Ben's relationship. She didn't think she could stomach watching them reunite so excitedly.

After she showered and had breakfast, she packed some things for the weekend into her duffel bag and then stopped to knock on Shaya's door. She felt that things had been a little awkward last night, but she wanted to say goodbye before she left.

Shaya opened her door and smiled when she saw Jexi. "Hi," she said.

"Hi," Jexi said. She shuffled her feet awkwardly. "Um, I'm going to head to my folks' for the weekend, you know, so that you and Ben can have some private time."

"I told you that you could stay and didn't need to run off because he was coming to town," Shaya stated.

"Yeah, I know," Jexi answered. "But honestly, I think I'd feel kind of like a third wheel. It was easier when Hunter was there to be a buffer. It's okay, really! But promise that you'll text me and let me know how things are going!"

Shaya giggled, "You should have told me you wanted to see Hunter! Ben could have brought him."

Jexi snorted as her cheeks turned a bit red. "NO! That is not what I meant! I just meant that it was easier having someone to talk to when you and Ben were all googly-eyed at each other." Shaya laughed and rolled her eyes. "Sure, okay. Whatever you say. But you have to admit, he's not bad to look at."

Jexi's cheeks reddened a bit more. "Well, um, I guess not." She began to backpedal. "I'm all packed, so, um, I'll be headed to Mom and Dad's."

"Will you at least stay and have lunch with us?" Shaya asked.

Jexi shook her head, "Nah. Thanks for the invite but Mom is making lunch. She and Dad have been whining about not seeing me much since we got back. I haven't even had a chance to share all of our cruise pictures with them. I'm looking forward to spending time with them."

Shaya hugged Jexi and said, "Tell them I say hello. When you get back Sunday evening, we'll pick out what you will wear to your interview. You can borrow something of mine if you don't have anything."

"That would be great, thanks!" Jexi said. "Have a fantabulous weekend!" Jexi walked out of the apartment and shut the door.

Shaya looked at her watch. Nine o'clock. She knew she'd better start getting ready so that she would be prepared when Ben arrived. She had so much that she wanted to get done. She quickly grabbed her towel and headed for the shower.

As Jexi was driving to her mom and dad's house, she began to feel that lurking sadness. As if she couldn't control herself, she turned in the opposite direction. She needed to see Brennan. As she drove toward the house that she and Brennan were supposed to share, an unfamiliar car pulled in front of her. She slowed down to allow them room, but she was barely focused on driving. She saw the house in the distance, and her heart skipped a couple of beats. The thought of seeing him excited her. She put on her turn signal to turn into the driveway, but the car in front of her did the same thing. What? Who is this? she thought. She slammed on her brakes and pulled to the side of the street.

Jexi watched as the car stopped in the driveway and a tall, slender blond hopped out and shut the door. Her blood began to boil. You've got to be kidding me, she thought. He's already seeing someone new? She observed the blond bounce to the door and ring the doorbell. Jexi was so mad; she could hardly think straight. However, she knew that if Brennan saw her car, he would know what she was doing so she punched the gas pedal and sped off. The blond turned around to see where the screech came from, but Jexi was already gone.

Jexi's heart was beating rapidly, and she was seething. She couldn't believe that he was already moving on after only a few weeks. Had he been cheating on her? If so, for how long? Who was that woman? Her anger overtook her, and she began to weep loudly and violently.

The next thing she knew, she was pulled into her parents' driveway. She really didn't remember driving there, but she was relieved that she had arrived safely. She wiped her eyes and blew her nose. She powdered her face a bit so it wouldn't appear as if she had been crying. She took a deep breath, grabbed her duffel bag, and walked to the front door.

Immediately after she rang the doorbell, her mother flung open the door. "Sweetie!" her mom exclaimed. "You never have to use the doorbell! Just come on in!"

"Thanks, Mom," Jexi replied as she looked toward the ground.

Her mom lifted Jexi's chin in her hands. "Honey! What's wrong?! Come in . . . let's talk."

Jexi flung her arms around her mother and released the tears that she couldn't hold back. She said between sobs, "He has another woman already, Mom! Already!"

Jexi's mom held her close. "Oh, darlin'. I'm so sorry," she whispered.

"What do I do now?" Jexi wailed. All of a sudden, she became aware of another pair of arms embracing her. She realized that her dad had entered the room and joined in the hugging.

"Oh, sissy," her dad said. "I know it hurts. I'm sorry. What can I do? Would you like me to pay him a visit with Ole Bessie in my holster? Your mom can bury him in the flower garden out back. She's been researching endangered flower species that would be protected from anyone ever digging them up. Nobody would know."

The thought made Jexi giggle. "Of course not, Dad. I'll be okay. It will just take some time. But thanks for the offer. I think I'm just going to go put my things in my room and maybe lie down for a bit, if you don't mind."

"Okay, dear," her mom called after her as she walked up the stairs. "We'll call you when lunch is ready. We're making your favorite, grilled ham and cheese."

"Sounds delicious, Mom. Thanks," said Jexi. "See you both in a bit. Love you." When she opened her bedroom door, she felt instant comfort. She really wanted to call Shaya but didn't want to interfere with her visit with Ben. Perhaps she would pray. Would God extend His peace to her once again?

She lay down on the bed and cuddled with her stuffed dog, Bingo, from her childhood. She stared at the ceiling. "God, are You there?" she asked. "Um, it's me, Jexi. Can we talk?" She paused and took a deep breath. She let it out slowly and continued, "I'm not really sure how this works. What do I need to do to get Brennan to love me again?"

She lay there in silence for a few seconds and then heard her phone chirp. She wondered who would be texting her. Maybe it was Shaya. She picked up her phone and saw it was from Hunter. What a surprise! She opened the text and read his message: I found this picture on my phone this morning and wanted to send it to you. God's beauty never fails. When the picture loaded, she saw herself, standing next to the rail on their sunset cruise. She was looking into the sky at the most breathtaking sunset. She remembered that moment, and her heart softened. She had no idea that he had taken this picture, but she had to admit, it was the best picture she had ever seen of herself. It must have been the background that made her look good.

She opened her text box and typed back, Wow, that is a beautiful sunset. Thank you for sharing this!

Her phone chirped again. The sunset isn't the only beautiful thing in that picture.

Jexi felt her cheeks flush. How in the world do I respond to that? she asked herself. She certainly didn't feel beautiful. She settled on a simple Thank you, but you need your eyes checked.

When her phone chirped again, she saw Hunter's response. My eyes have been checked and I have twenty-twenty vision. I've been thinking about how much fun we had on the cruise. I enjoyed spending time with you. Maybe we'll see each other again.

Jexi was at a loss as to what to say to him. She did have fun with him, but she was so confused. She typed, Yes it was fun. Have a great weekend.

She opened the picture one more time and was amazed at the gorgeous sunset. Was God really the artist of all that splendor? She put her phone on the nightstand and looked at the ceiling again. "What do I do, God? Does Brennan still love me? Did he ever love me? Please help me." She suddenly felt exhaustion consuming her body and mind. She closed her eyes and drifted off to sleep.

Shaya rushed around tidying the apartment. There really wasn't anything left to clean, but she was nervous and needed to do something. She had already showered and gotten ready. She was wearing a new pair of jeans and a sparkly pink top that she had gotten last weekend. She glanced in the mirror as she passed by with her dustcloth. She looked pretty good!

She moved the magazines and the Bible on the coffee table around for the hundredth time and she heard the doorbell. She froze and then glanced at her watch. Eleven o'clock. Could that be Ben? If it is, he's early! If it isn't him, then I need to get rid of whoever is interrupting my anticipation frenzy! she thought.

She yelled, "Just a minute!" She ran and threw the dust cloth into the laundry basket and then quickly washed her hands. "I'm coming!" she yelled as she ran toward the door, still rubbing in the lotion.

Shaya opened the door and right before her eyes stood Ben. Oh, boy, he sure looked handsome! He was holding a bouquet of flowers, a Pepsi, and a dark chocolate candy bar. Shaya melted inside. He remembered! she thought, as she hurled herself towards him, smashing the flowers between them.

"Whoa, hold on, let me get my hands free!" Ben said, laughing. He had nearly dropped the gifts when he was trying to hug her. He set the items on the ground, and they returned to the embrace. They stood that way for several seconds, just enjoying the closeness.

"I missed you so much," he whispered.

"I missed you too," Shaya replied.

They released each other and Ben bent down to pick up the flowers, soda, and candy. Shaya invited him in and they walked to the couch and sat down.

"You're early!" Shaya said in her fake mad voice.

"I know," Ben answered. "I just couldn't wait a minute more. I had to get to you."

Shaya giggled uncomfortably and reached for the soda. "Well, at least you brought me Pepsi." She took several swallows of the soda as they sat in awkward silence.

"What do you want to do today?" Shaya asked Ben.

Ben replied, "I thought you could show me around."

"Do you want to stay close to the apartment, or actually go to the downtown Kansas City area?" Shaya asked.

"I've never seen either," Ben replied. "So, you pick."

Shaya rolled her eyes. "Ugh. Okay." She thought about it for a moment. "Got it. Let's go to the Arabia Steamboat Museum. It's amazing to see all the artifacts that were recovered from a ship that sank in the mid-nineteenth century. There are also some good places to have lunch in the River Market area."

"I like it," said Ben. "I don't care where we go, as long as I'm with you."

Shaya's heart swelled, and her cheeks reddened. It was becoming increasingly more difficult to deny her love for this man. She regained composure and cleared her throat. "Let me put these flowers in water, grab my purse and keys, and we'll head out!"

CHAPTER SEVENTEEN

Sunday night found Shaya sitting on the couch and writing in her prayer journal. She had so many thoughts and concerns that she needed to share with God. Ben had been gone for about an hour and Jexi was due home at any moment. She needed this quiet time to process. The weekend had been magical, and Ben's departure had left her feeling empty and lonely. She didn't expect to feel this way.

Shaya was so lost in prayer and thought that she was startled at the sound of a key being put into the front door. She looked up and saw Jexi walking into the apartment. She noticed that Jexi looked tired and troubled as she dragged her duffel bag in and set it down.

Jexi shut the door behind her and looked at Shaya. It was almost as if she could hide nothing from her best friend and her eyes filled with tears.

Shaya patted the couch seat next to her and Jexi sat down. "What happened?" Shaya asked softly.

Jexi took a deep breath. "I think he's seeing someone else. And what's worse is that I don't know if he was seeing her while we were still together or not." As soon as the words left her mouth, she was sobbing again, just as harshly as she had been when she first saw the woman at Brennan's house.

"Oh, crud, Jex," Shaya said. "I'm so sorry. I know how much that must hurt." She really wanted to be there for her friend, but she was also bursting because she had so much to share about her weekend. She added, "How do you know? What happened?"

"On the way to my parents, I drove down his street," Jexi answered.

"Jex!" Shaya retorted. "Seriously?"

"I know, I know," Jexi said. "But I just wanted to see him. I thought we could talk. But when I got to his driveway, I saw a blond girl getting out of a car and going into his house instead."

Shaya resisted the urge to roll her eyes. She secretly wished that Jexi could just let go already. But she really wanted to be supportive. So, she let Jexi finish talking and did her best to understand.

Jexi finished telling her about her weekend with her parents. She giggled half-heartedly when she told Shaya that her dad had offered to take care of business with Ole Bessie and bury Brennan in the flower bed. All of a sudden, she stopped. "Wait!" she gasped. "I have been so wrapped up in my sorrow that I have totally been ignoring your weekend! I want details! What did you two do? Where did you go? Did you kiss him? When will you see him next?"

Shaya looked at her friend, who had red eyes and mascara running down her cheeks. She felt a little uncomfortable talking about her happiness when she could clearly see that Jexi was hurting. "We don't have to talk about that right now."

Jexi begged. "Oh, please. I need something to smile about!"

"Okay," she said, followed by a dramatic pause. "It was beyond perfect!"

Jexi smiled. "And?"

Shaya said, "We went to Steamboat Arabia. We ate several meals. We went to church. We went on a hike. We went shopping . . . ."

Jexi leaned closer. "Aaaannnd . . . ?"

"Oh, you want to know if he kissed me goodbye?" Shaya asked with a cheesy grin.

Jexi jumped up off the couch. "OF COURSE I want to know!" she screamed.

"Yeah," she said with a nonchalant shrug.

Jexi stared at her in disbelief. "That's it?" she asked.

Shaya jumped up next to Jexi and squealed, "AAH, it was perfect!"

Jexi laughed. "I knew it!" she exclaimed. "I'm so happy for you!"

"Thanks," responded Shaya. She sat back down and lowered her head. "But now I'm even more confused. I don't know if I can stand being away from him. I already miss him so much."

"So you need to make plans to see him as much as possible," said Jexi. "It really seems like this relationship is meant to be! Don't give up on it!"

"I can't help but remember how and why it failed before," Shaya responded. "I don't know if we can make a long-distance relationship work. Besides, where do we go with it? I mean, neither of us really wants to move. I just don't see how this is going to be possible."

"Have I ever told you that you worry too much?" asked Jexi. "Ben is obviously head over heels for you and it is so clear that you are totally in love with him too. You're both older and more mature now. Make it work."

Shaya looked up and smiled at Jexi. "Since when did you become the sensible one?" she said, teasingly.

Jexi grinned. "I don't know," she answered. "But something just tells me that Ben is THE ONE for you!"

"I do love him. But don't you DARE repeat that to anyone," Shaya said.

Jexi pretended to zip her lips. "My lips are sealed," she said. "May I make a suggestion?"

"Sure," Shaya replied.

"Maybe you should pray about it," Jexi said, sheepishly.

A look of complete shock covered Shaya's face. "Did I hear you say what I think I heard?" she asked.

Jexi scoffed and shrugged her shoulders. "Yeah, don't make a big deal about it. I just know that you like to talk to God and pray and stuff. I thought maybe that could be something you pray about."

Shaya picked up her prayer journal. "That's actually what I was doing when you got home," she said. "But thank you for suggesting that. You made my day!"

Jexi smiled. "Oh, I almost forgot!" she blurted. "Guess who texted me yesterday?"

Shaya looked puzzled. "I don't know," she answered.

"You'll never guess, so I'll just tell you," Jexi said with a bit of a grin. "Hunter! He sent a picture that he took of me on the cruise! It was super sweet!"

Shaya noticed that while Jexi was talking, her eyes seemed to twinkle a bit and her sadness seemed to lift. "What picture?"

Jexi pulled out her phone and showed her. "I had no idea that he even took this!"

"Wow!" Shaya replied. "He sure has an eye for photography!"

Jexi blushed. "It's no big deal," she said, trying to downplay the image. "You can read the messages he sent me if you want."

Shaya giggled. "No need, no need," she responded. "But it is quite interesting that he decided to take that picture and then send it later. It's a bit of a romantic gesture. It's almost like he had a plan."

Jexi gave Shaya a playful shove. "Oh, shut up," she said. "It's no big deal. I already told you." She looked at her watch. "It's getting late. I'm hitting the sack."

Shaya stopped her. "I get the hint. End of the discussion, but it's not that late. We still have to pick out your outfit for the interview on Tuesday, remember? You said you might need to borrow something of mine."

Jexi sighed. "Oh, right," she mumbled. "Okay. Let's go see what you've got."

Once the two picked out the perfect ensemble for Jexi's interview and giggled with each other a little more, it was time to turn in for the evening.

Both girls drifted off to sleep from exhaustion, albeit different types of exhaustion. Shaya was smiling and filled with confusion as she dozed off, but Jexi cried herself to sleep. Both were anticipating what the next few months might hold.

One hundred fifty miles away, Ben was falling asleep with a smile on his face as well. He had really enjoyed the time with Shaya. He wanted to get in his car and drive back to her at that very moment, but he had a job to go to in the morning. He was already thinking about going up the following weekend. "Heavenly Father," he prayed. "Thank You for bringing Shaya back into my life. I know You have a plan for us. I don't see the big picture and I am unsure of how this is going to work out. But, God, I am open to whatever You have for us. Lord, bring her home to me, please." He paused briefly. "Not MY will, but YOURS. In Jesus' name, I pray. Amen." He closed his eyes and drifted off into a peaceful sleep.

Across town in Baxter Springs, Hunter was falling asleep also. He could not seem to get his mind to stop thinking about Jexi. He wondered why she was stuck in his thoughts. She was obviously NOT emotionally available. He prayed, "God, I really like her. I know I've only known her for a short while, but I feel that she has an important place in my life. Please, make Your will known to both of us. Amen."

CHAPTER EIGHTEEN

Jexi aced her interview and accepted a job at the bookstore downtown. She was thrilled to be working at the store. While she was there, she was able to focus on work and even put Brennan out of her mind for a while.

Fall at the bookstore was filled with fun events and activities. Jexi was loving her job there and was so thankful for the opportunity. She had a passion for reading but never imagined having a career surrounded by books. She was able to view all of the new arrivals, plus she got an employee discount that tended to get her into trouble. She had already purchased more books than she would be able to read in a year.

The quaint bookstore was doing well, and Jexi was thriving there. It was currently quiet, so she was taking the opportunity to dust the shelves and straighten the books. Her hand stopped on a book with a stunning photograph of a beach sunset. She smiled to herself as she thought of her "honeymoon" cruise and the fun she had with Shaya, Ben, and Hunter. Hunter, she thought.

She was jolted out of her daydream by her boss and owner of the bookstore, Shaun.

"Jexi," he said, "I've been thinking about how we can attract more customers. You've proven yourself to be a valuable employee, and I have a project that I want to run by you."

Jexi nodded in response. "Thanks," she said, sheepishly. "What did you have in mind?"

"Well, we have all that space in the back that would be perfect for live performers," Shaun explained. "It already has a stage and is rigged for lighting. All it needs is a little TLC and then we can start having bands play. What do you think?"

Jexi thought about it for a moment and asked, "What kind of music were you considering?" she asked.

"All kinds," Shaun responded. "Well, all except the vulgar and inappropriate, of course."

Jexi liked the idea. "That would be great!" she responded. "I think that it would bring in a lot of new people! We could reach out to bands that are just starting up and also some more famous bands." She could feel herself getting excited about the idea. "What were you thinking that I could do?" she asked.

"Well," Shaun answered. "I was sort of hoping that you could be in charge of bringing in the talent. Do you think you would like that job? It would pay a bit more than your current position."

Jexi grinned. "Yes!" she answered. "I would love that! I can still work in the bookstore, right?"

Shaun nodded, "Of course," he answered.

"Great!" answered Jexi. "I can't wait to get started!"

Jexi was ready to rush home and tell Shaya the news. Life was turning out okay, after all.

As soon as she clocked out, she drove home and all she could think about was her exciting new job. She pulled into the parking lot and jumped out of the car. She practically ran to the apartment. She burst through the door and yelled, "Shaya! Shaya!"

Shaya rushed out of the kitchen with an oven mitt on one hand. "What?! What is going on? Who's hurt? Are you okay?" she cried in fear.

"I'm fine. In fact, I'm better than fine!" Jexi shrieked. "I got a promotion! Shaun wants to bring in bands and use the back room of the bookstore to have live gigs! He put me in charge of finding the talent! I'm so excited! Plus, it comes with a pay raise!" She sank down onto the sofa. Immediately she sat up. "But wait!" she said with panic in her voice. "What do I know about finding bands? Where am I going to start? I don't know any bands!"

"I am thrilled for you, Jex!" Shaya squealed. "That is wonderful news! But as for where you should start, don't you happen to know a guy in a band?"

"Of course not, Shaya," Jexi replied. "I don't know anyone in a band. I don't get to hobnob with the rich and famous, you know."

Shaya's mouth dropped open. "You're teasing, right?" she asked suspiciously.

Jexi looked at her skeptically. "What are you getting at?" she asked. "You know me better than anyone and you, of all people, should know that I don't have those kinds of contacts!"

"Duh, what about HUNTER?" Shaya asked.

Jexi sucked in her breath. "Ooh, yeah!" she realized. "I hadn't even thought about him!"

Shaya laughed. "You've forgotten about him so quickly? I guess he didn't make much of an impression on you!"

"Yeah, yeah, whatever," Jexi answered. "But you're right. I should see if he and Ben would like to come up and play. Shaun did say he would like to have all types of music. I just hadn't considered Christian music. Do you think they'd go for it?"

Shaya smiled. "I think they would very much go for it. I know for a fact that Ben loves to play and sing. I know Hunter does too. Give him a call."

Jexi's smile left her face. "No," she said. "You call Ben. You can see what he thinks about it."

Shaya snickered. "Oh, no," she replied. "This is YOUR new position, right? I'm not getting paid to bring in the talent, as you say."

"Really?" Jexi groaned. "You're really going to make me call Hunter?"

"Yes, ma'am," Shay retorted. "It's not like he is a complete stranger. Plus, it will give you good practice!"

"Fine," Jexi snorted begrudgingly. "I'll call him. But not tonight."

Shaya giggled at her. "Okay, big britches, dinner is ready. Let's eat."

The next day, while at work, Jexi hesitantly picked up her phone. She pulled up Hunter's number and stared at it for the next ten minutes. She was so nervous but wasn't sure exactly why. Would he think that she was crazy for reaching out to him?

She pressed the send button. The phone rang twice and all of a sudden, she heard Hunter's deep voice. "Hello?" he answered.

"Um, um, hi," Jexi stammered. "Um, this is Jexi." She immediately felt stupid. Of course, he knew it was her thanks to caller ID. She wished she could hang up, but she didn't. She had a job to do.

"Hey, Jexi!" Hunter responded. Jexi asked herself, Does he sound happy?

"Hey," Jexi said. "You're probably wondering why I'm calling." She began to launch into a monologue about the back room at the store and how her boss was wanting to bring in bands to play live gigs. She continued saying that their band would be paid for their time, but since the store was just beginning this adventure, it probably wouldn't pay as much as he was accustomed to. The store would handle all the promotions for them. She said that they could play one night or several nights. She started to mention that they didn't know an exact date yet, but she could let him know later when he interrupted her ramble.

"Whoa, whoa!" laughed Hunter. "Let's slow down. Of course, I'll play for you. Anytime."

Jexi blushed and felt grateful that he couldn't see her right then. "Oh, great!" she exclaimed. "My boss will be so happy that I've been able to get some interest. We don't have an opening date yet. Can I get back to you on that?"

"Sure," replied Hunter. "I just need a couple of weeks' notice to find someone to lead worship at church."

"Oh, sure, no problem," replied Jexi. "We haven't even really started on refurbishing the back room yet, so it will be a little bit yet. Thanks so much!"

"You're welcome!" Hunter said. "It will be good to see you."

What was this feeling fluttering in her stomach? She didn't understand why he could make her blush this way. Again, she was grateful this wasn't a video call. "Um, you too," she croaked out. "Okay then, talk to ya later!"

As she was just about to push the disconnect button, she heard his voice calling, "Wait, hold on!"

She put the phone back up to her ear. "Yeah?" she asked.

"How are you doing?" Hunter inquired.

Jexi was stunned by the question. "What do you mean? I'm fine." She could almost hear Hunter's smile in his voice.

"That's pretty vague," Hunter mentioned. "What I mean is, I'm curious about how you've been doing since the cruise. It sounds like you really like your job."

Jexi felt her cheeks redden once again. Has he been thinking about me? she thought. She felt it would be safe to talk about her job since he brought it up, so she decided to stick to that topic. "I do like my job," she answered. "I love working in a bookstore."

"That's great!" Hunter replied. "I'm glad that you're happy."

"Thanks," Jexi whispered. "Um, well, I need to get going. I've got to locate some more talent. Have a good day!"

"It was good to talk with you," Hunter said softly.

"Yeah, you too," Jexi replied quickly. "Bye!"

She hung up before she heard Hunter respond. She let out the breath she'd been holding. The only way she could describe her current feeling was confusion.

CHAPTER NINETEEN

The back room at the bookstore was ready by early November. It looked magnificent. It wasn't fancy, but it was sleek. Shaun was excited to have the bands start playing. He was proud of Jexi for having several bands lined up to play.

Jexi had not talked to Hunter since she had called to invite him to perform. Now that they had an opening date, she would need to call and get him scheduled. She was far more nervous than she should be to make the call. It wasn't like he was a stranger. She couldn't figure out why this man made her feel so peculiar. Jexi knew that she had to make this call today. She'd been putting it off but in order to give Hunter enough notice, she had no other choice.

She picked up her phone and stared at Hunter's number. She had added a photo of him to her contact list. With his face smiling back at her, she took a deep breath and pressed the send button.

Within two rings she heard the sound of his voice on the line. "Hi, Jexi! What's up?"

"Well, I have a date for you," Jexi responded.

"A date?" Hunter quipped. "Sounds interesting! When are we going out?"

Jexi cleared her throat and choked out a response. "Um, uh, no, nothing like that. I meant a date for your band to play at the bookstore."

"Oh, I see," Hunter responded.

Did he sound disappointed? Jexi wondered. She shook her head. She didn't have time to mess with those thoughts. She focused on the job at hand.

"We have the weekend before Thanksgiving scheduled for our grand opening. You would play Saturday night. You could also play on Sunday for a matinee if you choose."

Hunter's voice didn't sound as exuberant as it had initially. "That sounds great, Jexi. We would love to book that weekend. What time will we be playing? We'll need to come in early to get set up."

"Yes, of course," Jexi answered. "You can come as early as nine a.m. to set up on Saturday. You'll go on at seven p.m. We don't have anything else planned that day except for you guys, so the whole day is yours."

They hammered out the rest of the minor details and the conversation was over. When they hung up, Jexi felt relieved and sad at the same time. What was with this confusion that surrounded Hunter? She put it out of her mind and set to get back to work.

The next few weeks went quickly as Jexi continued to pursue local talent and book them into the back room. The grand opening was fast approaching and there was a lot to get done. It kept her at work late several nights.

The Thursday night before the grand opening of the back room, Jexi and Shaya were sitting at home watching television. It was the first night that Jexi had been home before bedtime since the opening date had been set. As soon as their show went to commercial, Jexi looked at Shaya hesitantly, "I invited Brennan to come Saturday night."

Shaya didn't even turn to look at her. She did her best to hold back the scream she wanted to let out but said nothing.

"Did you hear me, Shay?" Jexi questioned.

Through pursed lips, Shaya asked, "Why?"

"I want him to see how great I am doing without him!" Jexi stated with confidence.

Shaya sighed. "I know you are still hoping that you two will get back together, but seriously, Jexi. You're going to have to let him go. He's obviously dating someone else."

Jexi turned back toward the television. "I shouldn't have told you."

"No, that's not it," Shaya said. "We share everything with each other, and I'm glad you did tell me. I just see things from a very different lens. Your lens is still Brennan-colored. Did you call him, or did you text him?"

"Neither," Jexi answered. "I just sent one of the store flyers to him in the mail."

"Good," Shaya said. "This is going to sound harsh, but if you contact him now, it's going to make you seem desperate and a little pathetic."

"OUCH!" Jexi winced.

"We share everything, but we also tell each other the truth, remember?" Shaya asked.

Jexi hung her head. "Yeah, you're right," she said. "I just hate it when you're right."

The two went back to watching their favorite TV show in silence. Jexi was glad she had Shaya in her life, but sometimes she could be so annoying. It was especially annoying because she knew that Shaya was right about Brennan. Jexi knew in her heart that she needed to move on. Actually, she felt like she was slowly healing. She really did want Brennan to see how great she was doing without him. Maybe then he would want her back. Perhaps she wasn't over him quite yet.

At the next television commercial, Jexi had a question for Shaya. "Hey, Shaya? Can you help me understand something?" she asked.

"Sure, as long as it isn't about Brennan," Shaya said with a giggle. "What's on your mind?"

Jexi rolled her eyes. "It's not about Brennan," she assured her. "It's actually about another guy."

Shaya sat straight up, snapped her head towards Jexi, and raised her eyebrows. "Another what?" she asked.

"Don't get so excited," Jexi said. "It's nothing major. I was just wondering why Hunter confuses me so much."

"What do you mean?" asked Shaya.

Jexi explained. "Well, I look forward to talking to him, but I also dread it at the same time. I think he's trying to flirt with me sometimes, but I'm not sure. And what's so bothersome is the way he makes me blush so easily."

Shaya let out a long "OOOHHH! Interesting!"

Jexi smacked Shaya's arm. "It's not like that!" she insisted.

"It's exactly like THAT!" Shaya retorted. "You have a crush on him!"

"I don't! I really don't!" Jexi continued to protest. "I just don't understand what this feeling is. I'm confused! And I don't think my heart is ready to move on anyway!"

"You can keep telling yourself that. But guess what? You are mistaken. You have a major crush on our dear Hunter and I think it's fantastic!" Shaya exclaimed.

Jexi paused. "Nah, I don't think that's what is going on. I just, well, I just . . . ."

"Just have a crush. You can say it." Shaya added with a giggle.

"I can't," Jexi said. "I'm not completely over Brennan and I just can't consider another relationship right now. And let's suppose I do have a crush on him, what is the universe thinking, sending me a new man when I'm not over the last one? It wouldn't make sense."

"Hunter is a great guy," Shaya said. "You could do worse. But think of it this way. Maybe God, not the universe, sent Hunter to help you heal from your heartache."

"You really think God is involved in this?" Jexi asked.

"I KNOW He is," replied Shaya. "He is involved in every aspect of our lives. Including love." Shaya glanced at Jexi's wrist. "I see you are wearing the bracelet Hunter gave you."

"Yeah, what about it?" Jexi asked defensively. "It's a pretty bracelet, that's all. I don't see what that has to do with anything."

"It is pretty," Shaya replied. "But it also has significance. Remember what he told you when he gave it to you? He said you are a child of God and are royalty. It's true, ya know."

Jexi opened her mouth to speak, but Shaya continued. "And since you are a child of God, that means He is intimately involved in all of your business."

"So, you're saying that God knows what's going on and He knows what I'm feeling?" Jexi asked.

"Yup!" Shaya answered. "And so do I. And you have a crush on Hunter."

Jexi groaned. "But I'm not ready. Doesn't God know that too?"

Shaya busted out in laughter. "God knows EVERYTHING and, just because you might not think you are ready, God has other plans for you."

"Plans for me?" Jexi asked in confusion. "Why would He have plans for me?"

"Jex," Shaya said. "God has plans for all of us. We have free will to follow His plans, or not. But His plans are always best. Maybe you should pray about Hunter. The book of James states that if we ask for wisdom, God will give it generously."

"Is that what you mean when you talk about God's will versus your own will?" Jexi asked.

"Yes!" Shaya said excitedly. "He has a plan for every one of his children. His plan is superior to anything we can come up with because He knows us better than we know ourselves. He knows what we need. And He always provides."

"You've been really great about answering all my questions lately," Jexi said. "I've learned a lot. Thanks."

"Are you ready to go to church with me on Sunday?" Shaya asked.

"I think I am," Jexi said matter-of-factly.

"Sweet!" Shaya squealed. "I've been praying for this moment!"

Jexi looked sideways at Shaya, "Don't make it weird," she said. Both girls busted out in a fit of laughter.

CHAPTER TWENTY

The day of the grand opening of the back room arrived and Jexi was extremely busy making sure that everything was working perfectly. She was so excited about having a hand in helping create something so incredible. Customers had been in and out of the bookstore all week and the place was buzzing about the first show.

At ten a.m., as Jexi was adjusting the table centerpieces for about the twentieth time, she heard a familiar voice behind her. "Hi, Jexi," she heard Hunter say.

She turned around and saw him. And right on cue, that fluttering confusion bubbled in her stomach. "Hi," she responded.

Immediately, Ben and Shaya approached them, holding hands and spewing happiness. Ben looked at Jexi and said, "Hi, Jexi. Good to see ya."

Jexi nodded as Ben then turned to Hunter and said, "The guys are getting the gear out of the van." The two men walked toward the stage to start setting up.

Shay reached for Jexi's hand. "How can I help you?" she asked.

Jexi jumped into action. "There is so much to get done. Are you sure you're willing to help?" she asked.

"Put me in, coach," Shaya replied.

Jexi showed Shaya the list of all the things that needed to be checked and completed. "Pick one," she told Shaya.

For the next few hours, the room was a flurry of activity. By four o'clock, Shaya announced to the group, "Guys, we worked through lunch. I am starving. Would anyone be interested in something to eat?"

"YES!" shouted all five members of the band simultaneously.

Shaun offered to order pizza for the entire gang and invited everyone to sit down for a break until it arrived.

Jexi sank into a chair. "Wow! I had no idea how hard setting up for a gig would be!" she exclaimed. "Thank you for your help, y'all!"

Shaun looked around the room. "This place looks amazing! I can't wait to hear you, guys, play tonight," he said.

Jexi sat up, "They are really good, Shaun," she said. "You're going to enjoy it."

Hunter grinned. "Thank you for the compliment!" he stated.

There was that blush again! Good grief, what is my problem? Jexi thought. She nodded at him and then looked at the ground.

Jexi relaxed when Shaya spoke up. "She's right! And I'm not just saying that because I'm dating the bass player." Everyone laughed and Ben winked at Shaya.

After the group had eaten and made the finishing touches, the band took the stage to warm up and do a final sound check.

"Let's take a walk," Shaya suggested to Jexi.

Jexi began to protest. "I don't really have time for a walk."

Shaya turned her friend towards the door. "Everything is done, and we need some air."

Jexi followed Shaya out the door. "Do you really think we should be leaving right now? It's almost showtime."

"Just walk," Shay said.

"Bossy much?" Jexi asked sarcastically, but continued to walk with her.

The two turned left out of the building and began walking on the sidewalk. The evening air was brisk, and the sun was setting. Jexi took a deep breath and let it out slowly. "I hate it when you are right," she muttered.

"Better?" Shaya asked with one eyebrow raised.

"Better," Jexi answered. "How did you know I needed some air?"

Shaya looked at Jexi incredulously. "Seriously? How do I know? Um, hello, Einstein, we are best friends, remember? I read you like one of the books in your bookstore!"

Jexi rolled her eyes. "Oh, whatever!" But inside, Jexi was welcoming the breather. Having Hunter there was doing a number on her stomach, and she was worried she might throw up. The crisp, fresh air was calming her.

Shaya looked at her. "It's okay, you know."

"What's okay?" Jexi asked quizzically.

"To admit that you have a crush on him," Shaya answered.

Jexi glanced at her and just muttered, "Oh, shut up," and walked back toward the shop.

"That's not a very nice way to talk to your best friend, who is trying to HELP you, by the way!" Shaya said, with a smile.

"Oh, alright," Jexi conceded. "Thank you. But I'm not admitting anything."

A smug look covered Shaya's face. "Okay, whatever you say." She followed Jexi back into the store.

At six p.m. Shaun opened the doors. People had lined up around the block and Jexi was thrilled that so many had turned up. She was a little worried that they would exceed their capacity of sixty people! She bustled around the shop, helping customers find books they were looking for and before she knew it, she heard the music start to play.

She helped the last customer finish up and then rushed into the back room just as Hunter's voice filled the space. It was as deep and velvety as she remembered it, and she got goosebumps on her arms. She was absolutely mesmerized.

In the center of the stage, the band had placed a wooden cross. It was draped with a brilliant purple cloth. She immediately noticed the sash and then looked down at her bracelet. She couldn't help but remember Hunter's words about her being royalty. Could that possibly be true? If so, that would be really cool. Shaya sidled up next to Jexi and the two listened to the songs tell of a generous and loving God who cares deeply about His children. Halfway through the show, Hunter stopped to talk about how God wants a relationship with each of them.

His words caught Jexi's attention. "John three sixteen states that God loved the world so much that He sent His one and only Son to die for us. That means you and me. His Son had to endure an excruciating and torturous death so that you and I can be free. No other 'god' can say that they have done that for their people. Our God is the one and only true God. He loves you. Follow Him and have an everlasting life."

Jexi thought about what he said. The words he used gripped her soul. Jesus' death was excruciating and torturous? She hadn't really considered that before. She remembered her parents telling her that Jesus died and rose again but realizing that it was a terrible and painful death made her see things a little bit differently. *Is Hunter saying that Jesus endured that pain for me?* she pondered. *I'll have to ask Shaya about that later.*

Shaya could tell that Jexi was deep in thought. What Hunter said had struck a nerve, for sure. She sent up a silent prayer, "Father, keep working on Your daughter. She is so close to realizing how much You love her."

Jexi and Shaya enjoyed the remainder of the evening, and both had huge smiles on their faces when it was over. Hunter closed the event in prayer and asked if anyone wanted to come to the altar and receive Jesus.

Jexi's heart leaped a little. She felt pulled to walk to the front but just as she started to take a step, Shaun approached her. "Jexi, you did a fabulous job on this event. Our book sales were higher than ever today and we made a little extra with this crowd. Every seat is full!"

"Thanks, Shaun," Jexi responded. "Let's hope the next one turns out to be just as successful."

The band finished, the crowd dispersed, and soon Shaun was able to lock the doors. Shaun congratulated the band on such a successful show and told them he looked forward to the matinee show the next day. "When Jexi mentioned you were a Christian band, I wasn't sure we would get any patrons. I was pleasantly surprised by the turnout!"

"To God be the glory," Hunter replied, simply.

Jexi furrowed her brows. "What do you mean? You were the one on stage, playing and singing," she stated.

Hunter smiled. "Yes, I was, but without God, I wouldn't have the ability to sing and play for Him," he said.

Jexi was a bit confused but decided not to pursue the issue any further. She could ask Shaya about it later. *I might need to start a list of questions*, she thought with amusement.

The band left their gear at the bookstore since they were playing the next day and made their way toward the van. They were all tired and ready to get some sleep.

Ben and Shaya hugged and kissed goodbye. Jexi looked at Hunter and gave a little wave. She didn't want to get caught up in a confusing moment, so she quickly walked to the car. Several minutes later, Shaya appeared and got into the passenger seat.

"Why did you take off so quickly?" Shaya asked.

"It's been a long day and I'm really tired. Let's go home and get some rest," Jexi replied.

Shaya nodded. "Yeah, as excellent as the show was, it has been a long day. I'm proud of you. You did a great job."

Jexi started the car and put it in gear. "Thanks," she said as she yawned. She pointed the car in the direction of home. She was more confused than ever.

CHAPTER TWENTY-ONE

Jexi pulled her wheeled duffle bag into the living room and hollered to Shaya. "I'm packed and ready! What is taking you so long?" she asked.

Shaya emerged from her bedroom dragging a bulging suitcase behind her. Her breathing was labored. "I . . . couldn't get . . . get it to zip," she huffed.

"It's just for a few days. What on earth do you have in that bag?" Jexi asked.

"Ben and I have a couple of special dates planned. I had to pack multiple outfit options," Shaya remarked.

"So, now we don't have a reason to go shopping?" Jexi asked with a giggle.

Shaya looked at her sideways, "Oh, we will still go shopping," she said.

Jexi laughed out loud and said, "Maybe you will need to buy a bigger suitcase!"

"Ha, ha, smarty-pants," Shaya said snarkily. "Come on, let's get the car loaded up."

"Are you sure your mom won't mind me tagging along for Thanksgiving?" Jexi asked.

Shaya snickered. "Are you kidding? She will be thrilled to have you. She's always pestering me about how I never come home enough. It's like she misses me or something. Plus, my siblings won't be able to make it this year, so you will help fill the void." She turned back to Jexi. "How are your parents feeling about you not being home for Thanksgiving?"

Jexi tossed her duffel bag into the back seat and shut the door. "They didn't mind. They are taking a trip to historic Pennsylvania to visit some family. It's like my mom's distant cousin or some weird, twice removed, something or other. I don't know. They said I could go with them, but I didn't feel like going."

"I'm glad you are going with me. We will make it a fun weekend," Shaya said.

The two climbed into the front seats of Shaya's car and pulled on their seatbelts. "Baxter Springs, here we come," Jexi said with excitement. "Hey, will I get to meet your dad?"

Shaya laughed, "Doubtful! I haven't seen him in so long, I feel like I have to meet him first," she replied.

After a three-hour drive, they pulled into Shaya's mom's driveway at about three-thirty p.m. Shaya's mom ran out to greet them and gave them both hugs. "I'm so happy that you are here!" she said.

"It's good to see you, Ms. Clark," Jexi replied.

"Oh, you stop it with that Ms. Clark business," Attie demanded. You call me Attie, like everyone else."

Suitcases were hauled into the house and the girls' noses were greeted with heavenly aromas. They dropped their bags at the door and wandered into the kitchen.

"It smells delicious in here, Attie," said Jexi as she looked around.

"Thank you, sweetie," she replied to Jexi. "Your Aunt Katie will be here later this afternoon," Attie told Shaya.

"Yay!" Shaya exclaimed. "I love Aunt Katie!"

"She has been refurbishing the apartment above the cafe. It hasn't been used in years. She thinks she might be able to rent it out for a little extra income," Attie told the girls. "I told her to not bother, but you know how sisters are."

Shaya turned to Jexi, "You will LOVE the food at Aunt Katie's cafe. It is the best home cooking you will ever eat."

Attie sucked in a gasp and squared off with Shaya.

"Except for yours, Mama, of course!" Shaya recovered. "I meant the best she could get from a formal establishment."

"Well, she is using my mama's recipes, just like I do. It does taste good!" Attie agreed.

By now, all three ladies were giggling and catching up on the latest in each other's lives. Shaya felt so good being back home with her mom and having Jexi there to share it was even better.

After some time, the girls went to the room they would be sharing. While Jexi settled in, Shaya grabbed her phone. "I need to let Ben know I'm in town. He'll be worrying if he doesn't hear from me soon."

Jexi stood up. "And that is my cue to leave. I'll go hang out with your mom so you two can get all lovey-dovey," she said sarcastically. As she walked out the door, Shaya threw a pillow at her. Jexi closed the door just in time for the pillow to hit the door and fall to the floor.

Shaya sat on one of the beds and dialed Ben's number. He answered before the second ring. "Hiya, gorgeous," he said. "Have you made it into town yet?"

"Yep," Shaya answered. "We got here about an hour ago. We have been talking with Mom."

"Sounds nice," Ben replied. "So, I've been thinking, since I don't have to work tomorrow, how about going out to dinner with me tonight?"

Shaya replied with hesitation, "Well, Jexi is here, and Aunt Katie is coming over in a bit. I'd hate to leave. But I would love to see you. How about you come over here? Mom would love to see you too! I think Mom was planning to start a game of gin rummy."

Ben laughed. "Okay, sweetheart, that sounds good. What time should I be there?"

"If you want dinner, be here by six. If you don't want dinner, make that seven," Shaya answered.

"Your mom's cooking and your company?" Ben asked. "I'll be there promptly at six!"

Shaya hung up the phone smiling. She was excited about seeing Ben. She was also excited about spending time with her family. This was going to be a good holiday weekend.

She walked out to the kitchen where Jexi and her mom were, and standing next to Jexi was Aunt Katie! She rushed up to her and gave her a huge hug. "Aunt Katie, I've missed you!" she screeched.

Attie looked up from her cooking and scoffed. "Where was MY enthusiastic greeting?" she asked.

Shaya dramatically squealed, "Oh, MOM, I am so happy to see you!" She grabbed her mom from behind and squeezed her tight.

Attie smirked. "It's not great, but it'll do. Now get off me."

Jexi giggled. "You two are hilarious."

Aunt Katie laughed as well. "Jexi, you have no idea," she commented.

The ladies talked, laughed, and cooked for the next little while. Dinner was ready to serve at six o'clock, just as expected. Shaya was setting the table when the doorbell rang.

Attie looked up. "Who could that be?" she asked.

Shaya grimaced and said, "Oh, didn't I mention that Ben was coming over for dinner?"

Attie scowled and said, "How do you know if I've made enough food?"

Shaya snorted, "Mom, you always make way more than enough food! You could feed an army at each meal!"

Aunt Katie chimed in, "She's right, you know."

Attie relented. "Oh, fine. Let him in. You're lucky I know you so well and already figured he would be here."

Shaya feigned shock. "What in the world are you saying?" she asked.

Jexi leaned over. "She is saying that she knew you were going to have him come over before you even said anything. As a matter of fact, we all knew it."

Shaya glanced at the plates in her hand and counted them silently. Five plates! She looked at her mom and smiled. "Thanks, Mom."

Attie waved her hand in the air. "Just answer the door already. That poor boy is standing out in the cold."

Shaya handed the plates to Jexi and went to open the door. Ben reached out to hug her immediately. She loved the feeling of his arms around her. As she stayed there, she forgot about anyone else in the house. All of a sudden, she realized that her mom, aunt, and Jexi were watching, and she felt embarrassed.

"Um, you all remember Ben," she stammered.

The three ladies nodded with knowing looks on their faces. "Mmm-hmm, we do," Attie said.

"Hello, ladies," Ben replied. "Thank you for having me over for dinner. Attie, the chance to eat your home cooking was an opportunity I just couldn't pass up!"

"Son, get over here and give ole' Attie a hug," Attie responded.

The pleasantries were exchanged and soon the gang was seated at the table to eat. Jexi reached for the bowl of mashed potatoes when she felt Shaya kick her leg. She looked up to complain but saw the others' heads bowed and hands joined to begin praying. Shaya was reaching for her hand on one side and Aunt Katie was on the other side. She clasped hands with them and bowed her head also. This is new, she thought.

Attie quietly asked, "Ben, would you do the honor of blessing the food?"

Ben began in prayer. "Almighty Father, thank you for this food and for the fellowship surrounding this table. Please pour out Your blessings on the hands that prepared this delicious meal. Lord, I am beyond grateful to be reunited with Shaya and her family once again.

You are gracious and ever merciful. We love You. In Jesus' name, I pray. Amen."

The echoes of "Amen" filled the room.

"Dig in, everyone!" Attie said.

Throughout dinner, everyone was jovial and enjoying the time together. The after-dinner game of gin rummy was equally hysterical. Attie won two out of three hands.

"I am convinced that she cheats," complained Shaya to Ben and Jexi.

"I heard that!" yelled Attie. "And I do not cheat. I am simply skilled in the ways of card playing."

"That's her way of saying that she cheats," said Shaya. The room exploded in laughter.

"Young lady, you are not too big for a spanking," Attie said.

"It's getting late and a little too tense in here for my liking," Ben giggled. "It's time for me to get home anyway. Shaya, I'll see you tomorrow?"

Shaya nodded. "Yeah, tomorrow evening. Come on, I'll walk you out."

CHAPTER TWENTY-TWO

Thanksgiving morning was filled with the hustle and bustle of chatter and chores as the four ladies worked together in the kitchen. While she was setting the table, Shaya asked her mom, "Is Aunt Jessie going to be joining us today? Should I set a place for her?"

Attie laughed. "Your guess is as good as mine! You you're your crazy aunt. We never know when she's going to pop in for a visit."

Shaya looked puzzled. "Haven't you talked to her?" she asked.

Attie turned toward Shaya with a fresh pumpkin pie in her hands. "Not in several weeks," she responded. "Last I heard she was doing some missionary work down in Honduras. She gets so busy and sometimes doesn't have very good cell service."

Jexi's eyes got big. "Honduras?" she repeated. "She isn't scared to go to strange countries? I know I would be!"

Katie chuckled. "Not that crazy girl!" she answered. "She is up for anything. She has been to so many countries that I can't keep track. But she's doing the Lord's work, and we are proud of her."

"She left right after high school to start missionary work, and never looked back," Shaya added.

"Wow," mused Jexi. "She sounds so brave. I don't think I could ever do that!"

"Don't underestimate the Lord," Attie said. "His plans always prevail."

Jexi immediately felt uncomfortable and stammered something about needing to use the restroom. Once she had left the room, Shaya whispered to her mom, "She's really struggling right now, Mom. Pray for her, okay?"

When Jexi returned, the subject had been changed to Ben. What a relief! "What else can I do to help?" she asked.

"Will you put the dinner rolls in the breadbasket?" Aunt Katie responded.

The ladies finished getting the meal ready just in time to hear the doorbell ring. Within minutes, the house was filled with cousins, uncles, aunts, and friends. The laughter was loud, and the atmosphere was filled with jolly and festive feelings. "Dinner bell!" Attie shouted over the noise.

Everyone gathered at the tables and found their seats. They all reached around to grasp hands for the prayer as the doorbell chimed again. Everyone looked up from their bowed heads and glanced at one another with questioning faces. "I'll get it," said Attie and Katie's brother, Uncle Joe.

Uncle Joe opened the door and there stood Aunt Jessie. Attie and Katie squealed for joy. "Thank You, Jesus! We have missed you!" said Attie.

"We weren't sure if you were going to come!" added Katie.

"And miss y'all's down-home cookin'?" asked Jessie. "I decided to fly home yesterday!"

Joe smiled and hugged his sister. "We are glad to have you here with us," he said. "You're just in time for the prayer."

Shaya jumped up, "Hold on! Let me grab a chair and another place setting."

Once again, the group gathered at their seats and reached for each other's hands. Hesitantly, they all looked around for just a moment to see if the doorbell would ring. When it didn't, Joe said the blessing.

Dinner was loud and busy, but Jexi found herself enjoying the atmosphere. She missed her parents, but being here with Shaya's family was just what she needed to find deeper healing. She wasn't sure what it was about them, but she felt different here.

After dinner, the men turned on the television to watch football and the ladies headed toward the kitchen to clean up. The chatter continued as the dishes were washed and linens were put into the washer. The ladies looked around the cleaned-up kitchen and released a collective sigh. "It's a lot of work, but so worth it," said Jessie.

Attie looked at her with bewilderment. "What work? Cleaning up is the easiest task. You should have been here early this morning if you want to talk about work!"

Jessie laughed as she gave her oldest sister a hug. "I love you, sis."

Attie softened slightly. "I love you too, but you seem to have a knack for getting out of the hard work."

"What can I say? I'm just smart that way," Jessie replied.

Although Jexi had been having a great time, she felt herself needing a tranquil moment to herself. She wandered onto the front porch. The air was chilly and brisk but felt good on her cheeks. She sat on the porch swing and watched a bird scratch for scraps. She wished she had a piece of bread to toss to the little thing. She considered going inside to get a leftover roll when she heard the front door open. Attie stepped outside and sat down on the swing next to her.

"You doing okay, child?" asked Attie.

"Oh, yes," replied Jexi. "I just needed a little bit of quiet."

"Yeah, my family can get quite rambunctious," Attie mentioned. "You sure that's all? Shaya has filled me in on what happened."

Jexi sighed. "Well, I guess it is all out in the open now. Yeah, he stood me up. Yeah, I wanted to get back together. Yeah, he's already dating someone else. But what's done is done and I'm ready for a fresh start."

Attie wrapped her arm around Jexi. "Hon, I know stuff like this is hard. I've had my fair share of heartbreak in my day. Shaya's dad just about wrecked me. But I put my trust in God and He brought me through to the other side of the pain. His plans are always better for us."

Jexi turned toward Attie. "Shaya has said the same thing," she noted. "Do you really believe that this could be His will for me?"

Attie took a breath. "God never wants us to hurt. And I don't know what God's plan is for you. But I can clearly see that what He is intending for you does not involve that man. He gives us what is best for us, not always what we want. Don't forget that you have family here to give you love and support."

Tears stung Jexi's eyes. Shaya's mom considered her family. At that moment, she felt so loved. "Thank you, Attie. That means more to me than you will ever know."

"We love you, child. And so does God," Attie stated as she gave Jexi a full hug. As they pulled away from each other, Attie shivered. "It's freezing out here! Let's get our crazy selves inside where it's warm!" She stood and reached for Jexi's hand. "Come on."

Jexi took Attie's hand and the two walked back inside. Shaya greeted them at the door. "What's up?" she asked.

Jexi smiled. "Not much," she said. "But your mom is an amazing lady."

Shaya giggled. "I already knew that, but I'm sure she doesn't mind hearing it again. Hey, Jex, come here for a minute. I have a question for you."

Jexi followed her into the bedroom. "What do you need?" she asked.

"Well, I'm going out with Ben tonight," said Shaya. "But I don't want to leave you alone. Would you like me to see if Hunter wants to join us and we can all go?"

Jexi thought for a moment. "No, thank you. If it's okay with your mom, I'd like to stay here with her and the rest of the family. I think it will be fun to get to know your Aunt Jessie. She's a hoot!"

Shaya grinned. "Yes, she sure is! I think she brought her craft supplies. You guys will probably spend the evening making some bizarre creations."

Jexi laughed. "Sounds fun actually! Plus, it's been a full day and I'm tired. You go have fun with Ben. I'll be fine here, I promise."

"If you are sure—" Shaya started.

"I'm sure!" Jexi said, cutting Shaya short. She turned toward the door.

"Wait," said Shaya and pulled Jexi in for a quick hug. "Happy Thanksgiving. Thank you for coming with me," she added as they walked out of the room together.

CHAPTER TWENTY-THREE

The girls slept in on Friday morning. While yesterday had been fun, it was certainly exhausting. Shaya had returned from her date at about ten-thirty p.m. and Jexi had stayed up talking with Attie, Katie, and Jessie.

"What should we do today?" asked Shaya. "Would you be interested in exploring the little town and stopping by Aunt Katie's diner for lunch?"

"That sounds fun!" said Jexi. "Although I ate so much yesterday, I don't know if I have enough room left for more food!"

"We'll walk it off and you'll be ready to eat once you smell the food at the diner. You thought Thanksgiving smelled delicious, just wait!" said Shaya.

Once the girls had prepared for the day, they went downstairs. They walked into the kitchen and saw Attie and Aunt Jessie sitting at the table sipping coffee.

"Good morning!" greeted Attie. "Would you two like some breakfast?"

Shaya smiled and hugged her mom. "Nothing big. We are going to Aunt Katie's for lunch." She turned toward Jexi. "How about a bowl of cereal and some orange juice?" she asked.

Jexi nodded. "Yep, sounds great," she answered.

The girls took their glasses and bowls to the table to sit with Aunt Jessie and Attie and began to eat.

Between bites, Shaya asked Aunt Jessie how she had liked Honduras.

"Oh, it was magical," Jessie replied. "I had a glorious time. The children are precious, and the people are so thankful. It's amazing how they can be so happy with what little they have. It really reminds me to be grateful for what I've got, that's for sure!"

"Is it really that bad?" Jexi asked. "Is the poverty that widespread there?"

Jessie nodded. "Unfortunately, yes. Honduras is one of the poorest countries in the world. There are so many people living below the extreme poverty line. So many residents live in houses that are simply mud walls with metal roofs. There isn't clean water, clothing, or enough food. Here, look at these pictures I took."

Jessie pulled out her phone and opened the photo gallery application. She showed Jexi, Shaya, and Attie pictures of her with children in Honduras next to small shacks or mud houses. There were pictures of terrible living conditions and malnourished people. Jexi noticed that despite their grim situations, the people had big smiles on their faces.

"I wonder what they are so happy about," Jexi wondered out loud. She didn't realize she had said it loud enough for others to hear until Jessie responded.

"They are smiling because despite being amongst the poorest in the world, they have the most valuable treasure," Jessie answered.

"Treasure?" Jexi questioned.

Jessie smiled. "Yes, treasure," she answered quietly. "They are grinning because they know that their sins have been forgiven by God and that the blood of Jesus has set them free. They are smiling because they know how their story ends. They are happy because they know that their current situations are not permanent. They are excited because they will one day be in Heaven with God! And that, Jexi, is the greatest treasure ever."

Jexi felt like she had been gut-punched. The empathy she felt for these people was overwhelming. She was so confused by what Aunt Jessie had just said. It didn't make sense to her that these people, who were clearly suffering, would be filled with such inexplicable joy and happiness. She was bewildered, but she had an urge to know more about what made these people smile. She had so much more in her life than all the people in the pictures combined, yet she was miserable. She only had fleeting moments of happiness that were usually drowned out by self-pity.

Silently, Shaya was smiling. She could see that Jexi was curious and wanted to learn more. She couldn't help but think that God was answering her prayer.

"I'll be sharing my experience with the church on Sunday. I'm praying for more people to join me in the mission field. Will you be there?" Aunt Jessie asked.

Jexi faltered. She didn't really want to go to church, but it would be hard to say no to Aunt Jessie. Plus, she wanted to learn more about the mission trips. "Yes," she answered. "I'll be there."

Shaya's face lit up. "Yay!" she exclaimed. "You're finally coming to church with me!"

Jexi looked at her. "Don't make it weird," she replied, and then the two burst into laughter.

Jessie and Attie looked at each other, curious about what the inside joke was, but decided to let it go.

Suddenly, Jessie spoke loudly. "I can't believe I forgot to tell you guys something. I have really BIG news! I have been taking online classes for the past several years and I FINALLY got both my bachelor's and master's degrees!"

Attie clapped her hands. "Oh, Jessie! I'm so proud of you! What is the degree in? Why didn't you tell us you were taking classes?"

Jessie hung her head. "I was afraid that if I failed, you'd be disappointed in me. You know what I used to be like; not finishing anything."

Attie clicked her tongue. "Jessie, you are so crazy. You have overcome so much. I have faith in you to finish anything you start!"

"What are your future plans, Aunt Jessie?" Shaya asked.

"Sweetie, I really don't know yet. My degrees are in counseling. I initially started the program to assist in my mission work. Those people need so much help and support to overcome their obstacles. I thought if I knew more about guiding them, I could be more successful," Jessie responded.

"That's really cool," Shaya said. "But using your degree for missionary work won't pay enough to cover the cost of your education."

"I didn't do it for the money," Jessie quipped. "I want to be able to help people. And I know God will provide for me."

"Speaking of plans," Attie said, "Besides lunch at Katie's, what else are you girls up to today?"

"I'm going to show Jexi around town," answered Shaya. "Probably some shopping too."

Attie picked up the girls' breakfast dishes and took them to the sink. "Well, you two have fun! Should I expect you for dinner?" she asked.

Shaya glanced at Jexi, "Probably not. I think we have dinner plans."

Jexi groaned. "You didn't," she said as she glared at Shaya.

Shaya pretended to be clueless. "I have no idea what you are talking about," she answered. "Come on, let's go."

Jexi rolled her eyes and followed Shaya to the door, muttering under her breath.

There was a chill in the air, but the girls opted to walk the two blocks to Military Avenue. After yesterday's meal, they both felt like they needed to burn some extra calories. The neighborhood was quiet with only minimal traffic. Some of the houses had already started decorating for Christmas, which brought a festive vibe to the small town.

"There are some places we can visit later that will require the car," Shaya stated as they walked. "But there is a new boutique in town that I want to check out. Mom says they have some cute clothes!"

Jexi smiled at the mention of shopping and cute clothes. "Good! I was starting to think there wasn't a single place to shop in this little town. How did you survive growing up without a mall or a shoe store?"

"Don't forget how close we are to Joplin," reminded Shaya.

"Oh, yeah," Jexi whispered.

The girls walked down Thirteenth Street and turned right onto Military Avenue. "This is Aunt Katie's diner," Shaya said as she pointed to a tall building on the corner.

Jexi paused her steps to peer into the window. She pressed her face against the glass under the sign that read Katie's Diner, in bright blue letters. She saw Aunt Katie rushing around from table to table and tried to wave at her.

Shaya laughed and said, "Come on! We'll see her soon enough."

They continued down the street to the boutique. Once inside, Shaya waved hello to Ginger, the shop owner. Ginger was helping another customer but waved back to Shaya. The girls browsed around the store. Jexi and Shaya both found a couple of shirts on sale. They chatted with Ginger as they paid and made their way back out into the cold.

Next to the boutique was a Christmas store, filled with all things Christmas. "Let's go in here!" squealed Jexi. "I love Christmas decorations! While they perused the store, Jexi found an ornament of a cute pig wearing a Santa hat. "I have to get this for Mom!" she exclaimed. "She loves pigs!"

Shaya giggled. "I love this store too," she said. "It opens every Christmas season."

By the time they left the store, they were loaded down with bags. "Let's stop by Aunt Katie's and see if we can leave our bags there. I have one more shop I want to hit," Shaya suggested.

When they entered the diner, Shaya found Aunt Katie in the kitchen. Jexi waited in one of the booths while Shaya talked with her aunt. After a few minutes, Shaya emerged from the back.

"Aunt Katie has a great idea!" said Shaya. "She says the apartment upstairs is almost finished and we can leave our stuff there."

As the girls returned from putting their bags in the vacant apartment, Jexi asked, "What is Aunt Katie going to do with that apartment once she's done fixing it up?"

"I think that she is wanting to rent it out," Shaya answered.

"That won't be hard to do," Jexi responded. "It is a very nice apartment! She has done a great job getting it renovated."

"There are actually two entrances to the apartment. The way we just went is one, but there is also an outside entrance at the back of the building. Did you see the stairs with the deck when we walked past?" Shaya asked.

Jexi smirked, "I was in the shopping zone. You know I didn't see no stairs!"

Shaya laughed. "You're not very observant, are you?"

Jexi shoved her friend. "Hey, leave me alone. I got excited about Christmas decorations. It can happen to anyone."

The girls walked across the street to see what styles the shoe store had for the season. Then it was back to the diner for lunch.

"I meant to mention it before, but this place is adorable. Aunt Katie has really made this place unique," Jexi said. "What are all of those things on the wall?" She pointed to a collection of various items.

Shaya laughed. "Oh, those are some of Aunt Jessie's projects. Remember, she is an avid crafter. She has been making things to sell here for years. It doesn't pay the rent, but it makes her happy and gives her something to do when she is not running around to foreign countries saving the world." Shaya picked up an ornamental birdhouse that was sitting on the shelf. "I think birdhouses are her favorite."

Once the girls finished eating lunch, they decided to walk back to the house and get the car.

"I guess I shouldn't have gone overboard buying stuff at the Christmas store," commented Jexi. "There is no way we could have carried those bags all the way home."

They drove back to the diner and loaded the shopping bags into the car and then Shaya gave Jexi a small tour of her little town. She took

Jexi to the schools she attended growing up. She drove by the famous bridge in town. She showed Jexi the park area around the river. She pointed out the corner where she lost control of her bicycle and ran into the stop sign. "I still have a scar on my knee!" Shaya complained.

Shaya then drove to the church her family attends. "Ben and Hunter attend this church also," stated Shaya.

"Oh, my goodness, look at that gazebo!" Jexi said as she pointed to a small gazebo on the top of a hill next to a large white wooden cross. There were trees all around that made the area appear so serene.

"Ben and I had a lot of long talks in that gazebo," Shaya reminisced. "He would hold my hand and just share with me his dreams. I've never been able to open up to another guy like I can with Ben."

"You are so lucky to have found him again," Jexi said, with a hint of sadness in her voice.

"You will find the right guy someday soon," Shaya assured her. "And it sure won't be Brennan!"

CHAPTER TWENTY-FOUR

That evening at six-thirty p.m., the girls were seated at Van's Steakhouse. Shaya had been really vague about their dinner plans, but Jexi had a hunch that she had invited Ben and Hunter to join them. The thought of seeing Hunter again gave Jexi mixed emotions and that scared her. She wasn't ready to have romantic feelings for someone else yet, but she couldn't be sure that what she felt toward Hunter was romantic. She was so confused, and she just wanted to run away. She was considering telling Shaya that she was going to walk back to the house, when sure enough, Ben and Hunter walked over to the table. Jexi's stomach felt as if it was turning in circles. Maybe she was going to be sick.

"Good evening, ladies!" Ben said cheerfully. He leaned down and hugged Shaya and then Jexi.

"Good to see you both," Hunter added with a dazzling grin.

Jexi gave a forced smile. "Hello," she mumbled. Shaya didn't know it yet, but she was going to get smacked later on.

The guys sat down at the table with them and picked up the menus. "What looks good tonight?" asked Ben.

"The two lovely ladies sitting with us at the table sure do," answered Hunter with a sly smirk.

Shaya groaned loudly. "Always the charmer, aren't you Hunter?" she laughed. Hunter just grinned.

Hunter then turned toward Jexi. "I'm glad that you're here," he said.

Jexi nodded but that was all she could do at the moment. Shaya spoke for her. "She has had a full couple of days and she's pretty tired," she explained.

"Let's order," said Ben. "Shaya, do you know what you want? How about you, Jexi?"

Jexi found her voice and softly said, "The rib eye looks really good. I think I'm going to get that."

Shaya echoed what Jexi said, "Yeah, me too."

Hunter said, "I think I'll get the rib eye also."

Ben laughed. "Well, that sounds like it's unanimous since that's what I'm going to get too!"

The waiter arrived and everyone placed their order. Jexi had begun to ease a bit and was enjoying Hunter's playful banter. It was almost like it had been on the cruise.

The four of them chatted comfortably through dinner and Ben paid for the meal. As they walked out into the evening air, Jexi and Shaya both thanked Ben for his generosity.

Ben looked at Shaya. "Can I talk to you for a minute?" he asked. "Privately," he added.

"Sure," Shaya said and the two walked a few feet away out of earshot.

"I wonder what that's about," asked Jexi.

"I'm not sure," Hunter replied. "Let's take a walk up the street while they talk."

Jexi shrugged. "Okay," she said. After all the food she had eaten the last couple of days, the walk would be good for her.

"I noticed that you're wearing the bracelet I got you," Hunter said as they started walking. "You really do like it?"

"Oh, I love it!" said Jexi. "It's so beautiful. I wear it almost every day!"

"I'm glad," Hunter said. After a long pause, he added, "I've been thinking about you."

Jexi didn't know what to say in return. I've got to change the subject, she thought. I'm not ready for this kind of conversation. She looked at Hunter and said, "Thank you. How has work been going for you?" Real smooth, she thought. He's going to think I'm an idiot.

Hunter quickly took notice of the change of topic and cleared his throat. "Um, it's good," he responded. "There is a new building going up on Fourth Street and our company has been hired to do all the electricity. So that's been keeping me busy."

"That's great," Jexi answered. "I am still with the bookstore, and I love it. My boss even mentioned having your group up to perform again sometime."

"We'd be glad to," Hunter answered. "We had a lot of fun doing that."

"I'll let my boss know," said Jexi. She searched for what to say next. All she could think of was, "It's a chilly night out." She immediately felt dumb for saying that.

Hunter took his jacket off. "Are you cold?" he asked. "Here, have my jacket." He promptly put the jacket over Jexi's shoulders. She shuddered at his touch.

"Thank you," she said. "But aren't you going to get cold?"

"Nah," Hunter replied. "I'm not a big fan of wearing a jacket. So, it gives me an excuse."

Jexi laughed. "Glad I could help," she stated.

"When are you going back to Kansas City?" Hunter asked.

"Sunday afternoon," Jexi answered. "I told Aunt Jessie that I'd go to church with y'all."

Hunter's face lit up. "That's great!" he said. "Hey, just a thought. Tomorrow is our town's Harvest Fest. Our band is playing tomorrow evening after the pumpkin pie contest. How about you and Shaya come tomorrow? We can all hang out before the contest and then you can stick around to hear us play."

"Sure, that sounds like fun!" Jexi said. "I'm sure we can talk Shaya into it if Ben will be there."

Hunter moved a bit closer to Jexi. "I was also thinking that maybe after the band plays, you and I could go for a funnel cake together. What do you say?"

Jexi's nerves sprang to alert. Oh, dear, she thought. What should I say? I'm not ready for a date. But I do love some funnel cake. Maybe I can convince Shaya and Ben to come too.

"Um, I love funnel cake. Can I get extra powdered sugar?" she asked.

Hunter chuckled. "You can have all the powdered sugar you want."

"Sounds fun!" Jexi responded, smiling.

Back in the parking lot, Shaya looked at Ben, suspiciously. "What's going on?"

Ben stopped and turned to Shaya. He reached for her hands and held them both in his. "Shaya, you know how much I love you, right?"

Shaya took a deep breath. "Yes. Ben, you are scaring me. Are you breaking up with me?"

"NO! Absolutely not. As a matter of fact, I am never letting you go again. Which brings me to my question," Ben said and then added, "I have really enjoyed our weekend visits over the past few months. The problem is that it is getting harder and harder to leave each Sunday. I know it's a lot to ask, but would you ever consider moving back to Baxter Springs? I want to be near you every single day."

Shaya's heart fell. She knew this day would come. This is the question she feared most. When she left this town, she vowed she would not live here again. She had a good life in Kansas City, but she loved Ben with all her heart, which had to be part of the equation. "Ben," she stammered, "I can't answer that right now. There are a lot of things to consider. Will you give me time to pray about it?"

Ben pulled Shaya in for a long, tight hug. "Of course, you can pray about it. If you are willing to pray about it that means there is a chance you will come home to me."

Ben and Shaya walked toward Hunter and Jexi and the four began talking. While it had been a fun evening, there were a lot of confused feelings in the air.

CHAPTER TWENTY-FIVE

Shaya and Jexi met Ben and Hunter on Military Avenue for the Harvest Fest the next afternoon. The four had a fabulous time playing silly carnival games and riding some rides that they weren't sure were completely safe. Jexi hadn't been on a carnival ride since she was a teenager, and she felt a little nauseous after that last spinning ride.

Later that evening, they watched the pumpkin pie contest, where the winner was able to eat three and a half pies in the ten minutes allotted. "How are they not throwing up?" Jexi asked in horror.

Next, it was time for Hunter and Ben's band to perform. The group walked to the empty parking lot where the stage was located. The equipment had already been set up and a crowd was forming.

Ben kissed Shaya on the cheek. "See you in a little bit," he said.

Shaya smiled. "Himnifinimy," she mumbled.

Jexi gave Shaya a puzzled look. "What?"

"It means 'God be with you,'" Shaya answered matter-of-factly, without looking at her.

"It does not!" Jexi snapped back.

Ben laughed as he and Hunter walked onto the stage. The crowd cheered and Hunter invited them to bow their heads to pray.

Jexi leaned toward Shaya. "Himnifinimy?" she asked with eyebrows raised in disbelief.

"Shh," Shaya shushed. "They're starting." She bowed her head and closed her eyes as she listened to Hunter pray and added a prayer of her own.

Jexi took the hint and bowed her head also. She listened to the prayer and then found herself saying "Amen" with the rest of the crowd at the end.

The band played spectacularly, and the girls enjoyed the show. Jexi was not able to sing along this time because there were no screens with the lyrics, but she recognized a few of the songs and was able to join in with some of the choruses.

After the show, while Hunter and Ben helped with packing up the equipment, Jexi and Shaya went to stand in line at the funnel cake stand. "They better get over here before we order, because Hunter said he was going to buy me a funnel cake with extra powdered sugar!" Jexi exclaimed as the line slowly inched forward.

"Oh, he did, did he?" asked Shaya suspiciously.

"Oh, hush," Jexi protested. "It's no big deal. I like funnel cakes. Hunter said he'd buy me one. Quite simple if you think about it really."

"Hmm, hmm," Shaya muttered. "Doesn't sound simple to me."

"It's nothing, I promise!" Jexi insisted. She almost felt relieved to see the boys walking toward them, so she didn't have to continue the conversation. She waved emphatically to them. "Hey, guys, over here!" she hollered.

Shaya laughed as Ben and Hunter approached. "What's so funny?" Ben asked.

"Nothing!" Jexi quipped quickly. "We are just really wanting a funnel cake."

As promised, Hunter ordered a funnel cake for Jexi and requested extra, extra powdered sugar.

"Thank you!" Jexi expressed to Hunter as they walked to a picnic table to sit down.

"You're welcome," Hunter answered.

"Oh, look!" Shaya noticed. "The parade has started!"

The group watched the parade of lighted floats as they finished their funnel cakes. They cheered the loudest when they saw the float from Shaya's church go by. "They have enough lights on that float to brighten the whole street," Shaya commented. "But I love the theme!"

Jexi read aloud from the sign on the float, "Jesus is the light of the world." She pondered that statement for a minute and then smiled widely. She could almost feel the warmth of the light. "I get it," she whispered quietly to herself.

The last float of the parade passed by them at almost nine o'clock p.m. Ben noticed Shaya yawning.

"We'd better get you home," Ben laughed. "We don't want you falling asleep in church tomorrow!"

Jexi laughed also. "She does start to fade fairly early these days!" she teased.

Shaya playfully shoved Jexi. "I do not!" she defended herself. "Need I remind you of the all-nighters I had to pull in college prepping for exams?"

"And how many years ago was that?" Jexi prodded. "You are MUCH older now."

Hunter smiled at the interaction between the friends and then found himself yawning also. "In Shaya's defense, I am also fading quickly. It's been a great day, but probably best for us all to get home."

"Why don't we give you a ride home?" Ben asked.

"That would be nice," answered Shaya. "Thank you."

The drive to Attie's house was a quick and quiet one. In addition to being sleepy, everyone seemed to be deep in their own thoughts.

As they pulled into the drive, Jexi noticed that Attie's house had transformed in their absence today. The large pillars on either side of the porch had been draped in white lights from top to bottom. White lights followed the high roofline and covered every angle. There were lights around every window and door and the pathway to the house had been outlined as well. Jexi couldn't believe her eyes! "Your mom really gets into decorating for Christmas, doesn't she?" Jexi asked Shaya.

"Oh, yes!" exclaimed Shaya. "And she isn't done yet! I'm sure she'll put the yard ornaments out tomorrow. She absolutely loves celebrating the birth of Christ."

The four got out of the car and began saying goodbyes. Shaya and Ben hugged. "You're praying about what I asked you, right?" Ben asked her.

Shaya nodded. "Yes, I have been. I just don't have an answer for you yet. It's a lot to think over. You know I always wanted to get out of Baxter Springs. It's difficult to come to terms with returning. But I promise, I will continue to pray, and I am committed to you and to God's will . . . whatever that may be."

While Ben and Shaya talked, Hunter walked Jexi to the door. "I'm glad you came out today," he told her.

"Me too," Jexi said. "I had a lot of fun. And thank you for the funnel cake."

"You're welcome," Hunter answered as he looked into her eyes. "I'm looking forward to seeing you at church tomorrow."

Jexi blushed. "Um, yeah, me too," she muttered. "Have a good night," she said quickly. She turned toward Shaya and hollered, "Come on, Shay, it's cold!"

Shaya gave Ben another small hug. "Coming!" she called back to Jexi. She looked at Ben. "I'll see you in the morning." She ran up the sidewalk to meet her very nervous friend and waved at Hunter as he passed her on his way to the car. He didn't even glance her way.

Jexi and Shaya walked into the house without saying a word. They walked silently to the bedroom and began the process of getting ready for sleep.

As she was dozing off, Jexi's mind raced with thoughts. She remembered how Shaya told her about talking with God about her problems and decisions. *Could I talk to God right now?* she pondered. *Would He hear me?* She was not completely sure how her thoughts could make it all the way to the God of the universe. She was not even sure it was possible. She rolled over and whispered, "Shaya, are you awake?" She wanted to ask Shaya how this prayer thing worked. No answer. Shaya was fast asleep.

Jexi rolled onto her back and stared at the ceiling. Here goes, she thought. God, I don't have any idea if I'm doing this right or not. But Shaya is asleep, so here I am. I am sorry if I am bothering You, but I need to know why it seems that Hunter is flirting with me. Is that a question I can ask? He's just so adorable and I am extremely confused. What about Brennan? I'm supposed to be married. Yet . . . there's this cute guy who is NOT Brennan. Am I supposed to like him? Why am I excited about seeing him tomorrow? Ugh, this is so hard! Maybe I'm reading the signals wrong, but I think he likes me. So, I guess that's all I have right now. I hope You heard this. Do I say amen now? Amen. Oh, P.S. Please help Shaya. Amen. Jexi dozed off with a feeling of calm similar to the peaceful feelings she felt when she was on the cruise. Maybe there was something magical about prayer.

CHAPTER TWENTY-SIX

Sunday morning found Attie, Shaya, Jexi, Aunt Jessie, Aunt Katie, Uncle Joe, and his wife, Melissa, at church. Hunter and Ben led the congregation in the opening worship. Hunter prayed before Pastor Dave made his way to the pulpit to share the message.

Jexi took note that the sermon topic matched the float theme from yesterday's parade. Pastor preached about how Jesus is the Light of the World. She enjoyed getting more details about the meaning of that statement.

Pastor Dave started by reading Psalm one hundred nineteen, verse one hundred five, "Your word is a lamp to my feet and a light to my path." He expanded by saying that the Bible is God's living word. Everyone can find guidance in their lives by reading and living the statutes that God puts forth in the Bible. He said that by using the Bible and allowing Jesus to be their guiding light, people are able to make the choices and decisions that please Him. Without Jesus as the beacon in their lives, people make decisions that are destructive to themselves and others.

Jexi was riveted. She was surprised that she was actually understanding what the pastor meant. This is kind of what Shaya had been telling her about following God's will. Jexi wanted to know more! She felt an extreme eagerness about God's Word, that she had never had before and could not explain.

Pastor Dave went on to teach a second point. "Jesus' light does more than just guide us," he stated. "When we allow Jesus to shine His light in our hearts, He exposes our flaws and mistakes! Think of it as a flashlight, shining right at all the darkness." Suddenly the lights went off, and Pastor Dave switched on a flashlight. He moved it around the room, pointing at different objects. Everything the light hit was illuminated brightly.

Jexi sucked in her breath. I don't think I want all the dark in my heart brought to light! she thought. But she continued to listen.

The lights of the room came back on and on the stage was a black curtain hanging from chains on a rack. "When those shortcomings are revealed, Jesus can deal with the root of those issues," Pastor Dave said. "Once Jesus deals with the root of the issues, He can then break the chains of bondage!" Pastor Dave swung his Bible against the chains, and they fell apart dropping the curtain to the floor. A gasp filled the room.

"Our sins of the past and our issues hold us captive," informed the pastor. "We beat ourselves up over mistakes made. We hold on to shame that isn't ours for hurtful things done to us. We keep them secret, thinking that if no one knows what we have done or what has been done to us, we will be okay. But we are NOT okay! Jesus shines His light into the core of our problems and releases us from guilt, shame, hurt, anger, and more! Whatever it is that causes darkness in your life, Jesus is the way to get rid of it. His light is the only way to be completely free. Turn your Bible to John fourteen, six." There was a brief pause as the congregation flipped pages in their Bible. Pastor Dave continued. "Jesus answered, 'I am the Way, the Truth, and the Life. No one comes to the Father except through Me.' Also, in the eighth chapter of John, verses thirty-one and thirty-two." He again stopped for a moment so the page could be found in the Bible. He began to read again, "'Then Jesus said to those Jews who believed Him, 'If you abide in My word, you are My disciples indeed. And you shall know the truth and the truth shall make you free.' Look a little further in John eight to find verse thirty-six. Read it with me."

The congregants all read together, "Therefore if the Son makes you free, you shall be free indeed."

Jexi liked the thought of being free from past hurts. She really wanted to let Brennan go completely. She hadn't realized it until now, but he was a form of extreme darkness in her life. She couldn't see past the black that surrounded her past with him. She desperately wanted to be free. Could Jesus' light really be the answer she had been searching for? Shaya reached over and slipped a tissue into her hand. Jexi didn't know until that moment that tears were rolling down her cheeks. She squeezed Shaya's hand as she grasped the tissue and smiled up at her. "Thanks," she whispered.

"Point number three," Pastor Dave continued, "is that WE are called to share the light of Jesus with the rest of the world. Once we have been freed from our chains, God calls us to share that freedom with others so that they too can experience that same release. Matthew five-fourteen through sixteen reads, 'You are the light of the world. A city on top of a hill can't be hidden. Neither do people light a lamp and put it under a basket. Instead, they put it on top of a lampstand, and it shines on all who are in the house. In the same way, let your light shine before people, so they can see the good things you do and praise your Father who is in Heaven.' When Jesus' light gets into your heart, you shine for others! Sometimes, we don't even know the amount of light we offer to someone who is trapped in darkness." Pastor Dave smiled brightly and threw in an impassioned directive. "Now get out there and shine!"

Several congregation members shouted, "Amen! And Hallelujah!" to encourage the pastor's message.

Soon, the crowd settled, and Pastor Dave spoke deliberately and softly. "There are some of you in this crowd today who have been hurting. There are some of you who have made mistakes. There are some of you who are still being held in bondage by those old chains. If you want to let those chains go, accept Jesus as your Savior. He will break those chains. He will heal the hurt. He will forgive the mistakes. Now is your opportunity. Would everyone here today please bow your heads and close your eyes? With no one looking around, just lift your hand if this is you. Jesus is waiting for you to accept His light. We will be praying for you to boldly make that choice for Jesus."

Jexi bowed her head and opened her eyes to slits as she glanced around from side to side. She noticed everyone had their eyes closed tight. No one seems to be looking, she thought. She felt enough courage to raise her hand.

Pastor Dave waited for approximately thirty seconds and then spoke again. "Those of you who have raised your hands, we are so proud of you. We thank God for you! Everyone will pray a prayer of acceptance and forgiveness together, but if you raised your hand, listen closely to these words as you recite them. Father God," he began.

Every person in the room repeated the phrases after the pastor as he led them through the prayer. "I am a sinner in need of a Savior. I know that the only way I can be set free from this bondage is with Your light. Shine Your light in me and reveal my dark spots so that everything is made whole and new as I accept You as my Redeemer. Thank You for dying on the cross for my sins. Thank You for conquering death so I can be reconciled to God. I accept Your glorious gift of grace and love and yield to Your authority in my life. Amen."

Jexi slowly opened her eyes and peered at Shaya. She searched her face and wondered if Shaya knew what she had just done. She had accepted Jesus into her heart and was over the moon excited. She smiled brightly, with tears in her eyes. Only this time, they were happy tears.

Shaya looked at Jexi and wondered if she had said that prayer with the others. She saw the smile on Jexi's face and suspected that she had. She could hardly wait until the service was over so that she could celebrate with her friend. She hoped, anyway!

"Congratulations!" said Pastor Dave, as he closed the sermon. "If you would like any help in your journey with Christ, please do not hesitate to ask anyone on our staff. We all would be happy to assist! Have a fabulous week!"

Hunter, Ben, and the rest of the worship team took the stage and led everyone in an upbeat song as the people filed out into the lobby.

Shaya stopped Jexi before she could stand up. "Are you okay?" she asked her.

"Yes!" Jexi squealed through her tears. "I did it, Shay! I said the prayer! I accepted Jesus! What Pastor Dave said totally made sense and I just had to, you know? I could tell that I need to have God in my life."

Shaya squealed along with Jexi. "Praise the Lord!" she said. "That makes me so happy! I am so proud of you! Thank You, Jesus!"

The girls hugged each other. "I think I understand some of what you have been trying to tell me, Shaya," Jexi said. "Even though I still have so many questions!"

Shaya laughed. "You will always have questions, but you will also get a lot of those answers. Trust me, I'll help you. Wait right here!" Shaya stood up and went through a small door to the left of the stage. When she emerged a minute or two later, she was holding a book in her hands. "Here, this is for you."

"A Bible?" Jexi asked.

"Of course! This is where you begin. This is where you will find most of the answers you need. It's a gift the church offers to new believers," Shaya responded.

Jexi smiled. "Thanks!" she said.

Shaya shrieked, "Oh, wait until Ben and Hunter find out! They are gonna be so happy for you! And Mom, and Aunt Jessie, and Aunt Katie . . . ."

"Whoa, slow down!" Jexi interrupted. "It's almost as if you want to put me in a parade and show me off!"

"Sorry, it's just such exciting news!" Shaya said. "It's a great day when new believers make the choice to follow God."

"Who is a new believer?" asked Ben as he approached the girls with Hunter.

Shaya spun around. "Jexi!" she practically yelled.

Jexi blushed and said, "Don't make it weird."

Hunter immediately leaned in to hug Jexi. "Congratulations!" he said as he wrapped his arms around her.

Jexi stiffened for a second but then relaxed to enjoy the sentiment. It really was a day of celebration. She knew that.

Ben also leaned into Jexi for a quick hug. "That's great, Jexi! Congrats!" he said.

"Let's have a celebratory lunch!" Hunter exclaimed.

Shaya's eyes lit up. "Yes! And we can invite the family!"

Jexi looked at Shaya through narrowed eyes. "Um, shouldn't we be getting packed and headed back home? We both have work tomorrow," she mentioned.

Shaya laughed. "Nonsense! We have plenty of time for lunch, silly. I'm going to go catch Mom before she leaves!" She ran off, leaving Jexi alone with Hunter and Ben.

Jexi giggled uncomfortably. "Well, I guess we are having lunch," she said. "Where should we go?"

Before anyone could decide on where to go, Shaya returned. "Mom said we can all go back to her place to celebrate. She still has tons of food left over from Thanksgiving and she doesn't want to get stuck with it, especially if there is a reason to gather and celebrate."

Ben rubbed his stomach. "Alright! More of Attie's cooking! Let's get going already! Hunter, you're in for a treat!"

Jexi gulped. She wasn't prepared to spend more time with Hunter today. She thought she would have time far, far away from him to deal with whatever it was that she was feeling towards him.

Hunter sensed an uneasiness in Jexi. "Do you mind if I join you all in celebrating this HUGE decision?" he asked.

Jexi looked into his eyes and felt the fear melt away. "I don't mind at all," she said.

CHAPTER TWENTY-SEVEN

Since returning home from Thanksgiving, work had been crazy for Shaya. One of her coworkers had quit, without notice, leaving the company short-staffed. Shaya was being asked to pick up the slack, which was taking her to the brink of exhaustion. Every day was becoming more and more difficult. Shaya walked into her apartment on December first, after a very long day, and found an envelope on the floor, just inside the apartment door. She reached down and picked it up and noticed that it was from the management of the apartment complex. She was just too tired to read it at the moment. She tossed the envelope on the table with the mail and sank into the couch. Jexi was in the kitchen, preparing dinner. She appreciated Jexi picking up the slack lately because her late hours were preventing her from helping much around the apartment.

Jexi heard Shaya come in and sit on the couch. "Hiya, stranger!" she teasingly called from the kitchen. "Another long day?"

"UGH! I don't know how long I can keep this pace. They keep adding to my duties but have not offered any additional pay. I'm not one to complain, but this is too much!"

"Have you tried talking with your supervisor?" Jexi offered.

"Yes, and a lot of good that did," answered Shaya sarcastically. "She just told me that everyone is overworked and that we all just have to step up to help the team. What's for dinner?"

"Pork chops," Jexi replied. "With green beans."

"And macaroni and cheese?" Shaya asked hopefully.

"Yes, I can make mac and cheese," Jexi offered.

"Sweet," Shaya said. "Good ole comfort food. Can I help?"

Jexi poked her head out of the kitchen and into the living room. "Nah, I got it," she said. "You just hang for a few and dinner will be ready in a bit."

Shaya gladly obliged and pulled out her cell phone. She hadn't talked with Ben all day and wanted to text him to let him know that she was home from work. She then set the phone down on the end table next to her.

When Jexi announced dinner was ready, she was met with silence. She peeked around the corner and saw that Shaya was asleep. "Poor thing," she said out loud. "I'll let her sleep." She returned to setting the table and heard Shaya's phone ringing.

Shaya opened her eyes and groggily reached for her phone to check the caller ID. "Pastor Dave? Why is Pastor Dave calling?" She sat up straighter and shook off the sleep. "Hello?"

Jexi busied herself in the kitchen, so she didn't seem like a busybody, but she was also curious.

Shaya ended the call and sauntered into the kitchen. "Sorry, I didn't mean to fall asleep. Is dinner cold?"

"You needed it," Jexi responded. "It isn't too cold. Just pop your plate in the microwave for thirty seconds or so and you'll be good to go. You weren't out for very long."

Shaya reached for her plate and placed it in the microwave. "Jex, I really appreciate all you have been doing lately."

"Happy to help," Jexi answered. "But are you going to tell me what Pastor Dave wanted or leave me hanging?"

Shaya giggled as the microwave beeped to indicate that her dinner was done. She opened the door and pulled her plate out. "Do you need to put your plate in?" she asked Jexi.

Jexi looked at her incredulously as she placed her plate into the microwave, "Yes, I do. And start talking."

"Oh, he wanted to offer me a job in Baxter Springs," Shaya responded and nonchalantly added a little shrug. She sat down at the table and started eating her dinner.

Jexi stopped punching in the numbers to heat up her food and whipped around to face Shaya. "He WHAT?" she asked. "Offer you a job? What job? Did you apply for a job at the church? Are you going to take it?"

Shaya held up a hand to Jexi as she took a bite of pork chop. She chewed slowly and methodically.

Jexi grunted and turned to finish heating up her food. "You're so annoying," she grumbled.

When her food was warmed up, Jexi joined Shaya at the table. "Why are you like this?" she asked.

"I'm hungry!" Shaya replied.

"Me too!" Jexi retorted. "Hungry for information! Come on already! Spill the beans!"

Shaya reached toward the bowl of green beans and knocked it over. "There. They're spilled," she said. She couldn't help but laugh.

Jexi tried to hold in giggles as she jumped up and grabbed some paper towels to clean up the mess. She handed some to Shaya as well. She couldn't hold her laughter back for very long. "Very funny," Jexi said as she burst into guffaws.

The two worked together to clean up the beans all the while laughing hysterically. Finally, the mess was taken care of and they sat back down to their meals.

"Okay, okay. The church is starting a Christian school and Pastor wants me to run it," Shaya finally said.

"That is so exciting!" Jexi said. "What an honor that they want you to run it!"

"Not really," Shaya responded. "I am stuck in an apartment lease until March. I can't take it."

Jexi looked Shaya square in the eyes. "I am going to tell you something you tell me all the time. Pray about it. Maybe this is a door God is opening for you!"

Shaya took a moment to finish her bite before responding. "I'll pray. That's a given. But right now, I'm too tired to think, much less be excited. I honestly don't see how it will work out. I know it's not up to me to figure out the details, but the lease is a legal agreement, and I don't have the money to pay to get out of it. I'm kind of stuck."

"If it is meant to be, God will make a way, right?" countered Jexi. "But I get that you're too tired to think about it tonight. We can talk more over the weekend."

Shaya smiled at Jexi. "I have taught you well, grasshoppah."

Jexi pressed her hands together and put them in front of her chest and bowed toward Shaya. "You are a very good sensei," replied Jexi. The girls giggled.

Shaya got up and put her plate in the dishwasher. She got out a few containers for the food they didn't eat. The two worked together to clean up the kitchen. "I hate to eat and run," Shaya said, "But I am so tired. I need to go to give Ben a quick call and get to bed. I have to start early tomorrow. Would you mind?"

"Not at all," replied Jexi. "Good night!"

By the end of the week, both girls were ready for a break. Shaya had been working a ton of hours and Jexi had been picking up the slack at home, in addition to working her own job.

Friday evening, Jexi went through the mail. She noticed the envelope from the apartment complex addressed to Shaya and reminded her of it. Shaya took the envelope from Jexi and opened it. Her face went ashen as she handed the letter to Jexi to read.

A look of shock crossed Jexi's face as she read out loud, "The building has been sold. Tenants will need to vacate the premises by midnight on December thirty-first."

NEW BEGINNINGS—NOT MY WILL • 183

There was silence for a few moments while the girls processed the information. Jexi spoke first, albeit in a whisper. "What are we going to do?"

"Well, you reminded me to pray," Shaya calmly replied. "I guess I'm going to move back to Baxter Springs and run a Christian school.

"How can you stay so calm?" Jexi asked. "I am out of a home, as of the end of the month! I'm glad you've got a place to go and something to do, I really am! But I am also sort of worried about myself."

Shaya slowly turned to Jexi. "Come with me," she said.

"Come with you?" Jexi parroted. "Um, and do what? And stay where?"

"Mom would let you stay with us. There is plenty of room in that big house of hers," Shaya said.

"I suppose that takes care of living arrangements, but I will need income," Jexi reminded Shaya.

Shaya gave a sly smile. "Pray about it."

Jexi stuck her tongue out at Shaya. "Cute." "Seriously, Jex, you won't need to worry about it for a while. Mom will let us stay there and you won't need to pay for anything right away. Your car is paid for so, really, all you have is insurance," Shaya explained.

Jexi looked at Shaya. Her friend was right. But leaving Kansas City felt so permanent. She wasn't sure that she wanted to leave her parents. "I actually do have to pray about it," she told Shaya. "I have no idea what I should do."

Shaya walked toward Jexi and grasped her hand. "Let's pray right now," she suggested.

Jexi agreed. "Yeah, I need all the help I can get on this one!"

Shaya said a very pertinent and powerful prayer and Jexi agreed with everything. Shaya asked God to give Jexi direction and to help Jexi see what door was being opened and what door was being closed to her at the moment. She prayed that God would reveal His will to

Jexi and that Jexi would have the courage to go where He leads. When Shaya said "Amen" Jexi echoed it and the girls hugged.

"What do you think?" Shaya asked. "Wanna come to Baxter Springs with me?"

"Temporarily," Jexi replied. "Just until I can get on my feet. After that, I suppose I'll go where God leads me, right?"

Shaya turned around and grabbed her phone. "I suppose I need to call Mom to let her know WE are moving home." She paused for a moment and winked at Jexi. "And then I need to call Pastor Dave to accept the position. And tell Ben." A smile lit up her face. She was going to be close to Ben.

Shaya could feel her heart leap in circles at the prospect of being near Ben again. She knew without any doubt that this was God's will for her. Everything had fallen into place so quickly and flawlessly. She knew that Ben was her future.

As soon as she relayed the news, Shaya's mom cut her call off abruptly and stated, "Let me call you right back."

Shaya held her phone out, with a puzzled look on her face. "That was weird," she said out loud.

"What's up?" Jexi asked.

"I have no idea," Shaya replied.

CHAPTER TWENTY-EIGHT

Later that night, Shaya received a phone call back from her mother. As soon as she hung up, she ran to knock on Jexi's door.

"Jexi!" she called.

Jexi opened the door. "What?" she asked.

"So, you know how mom was all weird about just ending our call earlier? I know why now! She called Aunt Katie. Remember that apartment she was renovating over the diner? She said that we can stay there! Rent free! Well, rent free for a few months, anyhow. Oh, and she has a job for you in the diner if you are interested. Have you been praying?"

Jexi nodded in surprise. "Of course, I've been praying. I just didn't expect anything to come of it on the same night!"

"Sometimes God works things out before we even ask," Shaya said.

"Wow," Jexi replied. "Well, all that's left is to talk with my parents and quit my job at the bookstore. I guess I need to give them a call!"

Jexi picked up her phone and dialed her parents' number. Her father picked it up after the fourth ring. "Hello, kiddo," he answered. "How are you doing?"

"I'm good, Dad," answered Jexi. "Do you and Mom have some time to chat? I need to talk with you about something."

"Sure, honey!" said her dad. "Let me get your mom in here and we'll put you on speaker. Hang on."

Jexi waited while she heard her father yell for her mother to come into the living room. She heard the change in the phone receiver sound as her dad put the call on speakerphone. "Hi, Jexi!" said her mother. Her voice was full of worry. "I'm here! What is going on? Are you in trouble? Do you need help?"

Jexi laughed. "No, Mom, I'm fine. I just want to ask your thoughts about the idea of me moving away from KC." She hesitated and waited for her parents to object.

Her mother cleared her throat and said, "I guess that depends on where you would be moving to, and who you would be with, I suppose."

Jexi explained all of Shaya's situation with her current job, her new job offer, and the apartment. She said that she would be going with Shaya to Baxter Springs.

"I think that is a swell idea!" said Jexi's father.

Jexi's mother agreed. "Yes, honey, I think that would be a great thing for you. You would be getting away from the situation with Brennan and it would be like a new start. Shaya is so kind to offer to have you go with her."

Jexi couldn't hide her surprise. "I thought you two would freak out at the idea," she said. "What gives? Did Shaya already talk to you?"

"No, we haven't talked with her," said her father. "It's just that we have something to talk with you about also."

"What?" asked Jexi with panic in her voice. "What's wrong? Who has cancer?"

Her dad laughed, "You come by it honestly. Nobody is sick. We also have sort of a plan we need to discuss with you. We were worried how you might take it."

"Uh oh," Jexi muttered.

"Oh, it's nothing like that, dear," said her mother. "We sort of made an impulse buy a couple of months ago and have been making plans to sell the house."

Jexi interrupted her mother, "Sell the house?" she yelled. "What for?"

"Let your mom finish," said her dad.

"Yes, sell the house," continued her mom. "We purchased an RV and also bought a smaller house. We needed to downsize anyway. We are retired and all of you kids are out on your own and we don't need this big house anymore."

"R . . . V . . ." Jexi stammered.

Her dad spoke up. "Yes. We thought it might be fun to take the RV and do some traveling around the country."

Jexi chuckled. "This is not how I expected this conversation to go. I really expected you to try to convince me to stay. HMMM, I guess I have nothing to hold me here, for real."

"Kiddo, you will always have a home with us wherever we are," said her dad. "But it is okay for you to spread your wings and follow where God leads you."

"Funny you should say that, Dad," Jexi said. "Shaya said that this has all been falling into place like a puzzle that only God could put together."

Jexi's mom chuckled. "I agree with Shaya," she said. "God's will always prevails when we allow Him to take the reins. You're going to be just fine, Jexi. And we are always only a phone call away. We love you!"

"I love you too, Mom and Dad," Jexi replied. "Thanks for listening. We will talk soon." Jexi ended the call.

Jexi stepped out of her room to find Shaya sitting on the couch. "How did that go?" Shaya asked.

"Surprisingly well," Jexi replied. "They are selling the house and hitting the road in an RV. They are going to travel the country and were waiting for the right time to tell me. I guess they were worried I wouldn't be able to handle them leaving." Jexi laughed and shook her head in disbelief.

Shaya laughed loudly. "God is incredible!" she shouted.

Jexi had to concur with her friend. She was amazed at how seamlessly things had worked out. It was literally almost perfect. She would miss her folks, but she knew she could call them or video chat whenever she wanted.

The only thing left was to quit her job. She dreaded leaving the job she loved, but at the rate things were going, she was almost sure that God had something lined up for her that she would love even more.

"Looks like you and I are moving to Baxter Springs," she told Shaya. "I DID NOT see this coming." Shaya jumped up and down. "Yay!" she yelled.

"Have you talked to Ben or Pastor Dave?" asked Jexi.

"I called Pastor Dave first so that he wouldn't give my job to someone else," Shaya said. "He is very excited! Evidently, they were ready to get everything started, and the person they had lined up for the position had to leave unexpectedly. Ben mentioned I was praying about moving back last week at church, so Pastor Dave instantly thought of me for the position. I actually just got off the phone with him, so I haven't had a chance to call Ben yet. I need to do that right now! Do you mind if I step into my room for a minute?"

Jexi sat on the couch while Shaya went to her room to call Ben. She briefly considered texting Hunter to share the big news but quickly changed her mind. She didn't want to start anything that she wasn't ready for. Besides, she would see him enough when they moved. Instantly her stomach wrenched into knots. How in the world would she handle that situation? She heard Shaya's words in her head, Pray about it! and saw her new Bible sitting on the end table. She picked up her Bible and set it in front of her on the coffee table. It fell open to the book of Philippians in chapter four. Jexi's eyes looked and first observed verse six and then seven. She read it to herself, "Do not be anxious about anything, but in every situation, by prayer and petition, with thanksgiving, present your requests to God. And the peace of God, which transcends all understanding, will guard your hearts and your minds in Christ Jesus."

She sat back and closed her eyes. Present my requests to God, she thought. But what are my requests? What do I want to know? She sat in silence for a moment. Instantly she had a thought. I want to know how to handle the situation with Hunter. I want to know how I feel about him. Those thoughts gave her pause because Brennan was not the first thing she thought of. Interesting.

Shaya burst out of her room screaming incoherently. Jexi was jerked out of her quiet reflection. "What's wrong?" she urged. Then she noticed the excitement on Shaya's face. "Oh, that's a happy scream. Can you tone it down a bit, Screamy McScreamerson?"

Shaya screeched shrilly. "I'm just so happy!"

Jexi covered her ears. "That's fabulous, but your 'happy' is WAY TOO LOUD! Some of the old folks are probably in bed already."

Shaya stopped jumping and sat on the couch next to Jexi. "Okay, all I need to say is that in one day, my life went from dreadful to nearly perfect. I have a wonderful best friend who is going to move with me into a new adventure; an amazing boyfriend, whom I will get to see every day; and a job I have always dreamed of having. God is amazing! Have I said that yet? Pinch me, will ya?"

Jexi laughed. She reached over and pinched Shaya. "Ouch!" Shaya yelled.

"You told me to do it!" Jexi defended herself. And yes, you have said how amazing God is! And I feel the same way!" She decided to keep her confusion about Hunter to herself for now. After all, it was a minor inconvenience compared to all the major things that God had orchestrated. "My story isn't as exciting as yours, but this will be good for me. I need a fresh start and I'm excited!"

The girls looked at each other for a moment. Shaya spoke softly. "I'm going to make this weird for a minute." She paused and took a breath.

Jexi laughed. "You? You hate making things weird!"

"I'm trying to have a serious conversation here," Shaya said as she tossed Jexi a sideways glance.

"Okay, go ahead," Jexi said.

"Thank you for coming with me. It wouldn't be as fun without you," Shaya said.

"Well, to be honest, I want to thank you for inviting me. I was worried when you first told me about all of this that I was going to lose you," Jexi responded.

"Shut your face! You know that would never happen. We are besties for life. End of conversation," Shaya retorted.

Jexi snickered. "We have so much fun together. We are going to have a blast in Baxter Springs! That little town won't know what hit it!"

"Let's get some rest. We have a lot of packing to do tomorrow!" Shaya suggested. "Plus, I have a resignation letter to write and couldn't be happier about it." Shaya reached for Jexi's hand and pulled her up from the sofa. Before she released her, she looked up and said, "Thank You, Lord, for this incredible development in our lives!"

Jexi said, "Amen!" and the girls bid each other good night and traipsed off to bed. Both fell asleep with smiles on their faces as they dreamt about their future plans.

CHAPTER TWENTY-NINE

December twenty-second was deemed as moving day. Jexi had talked with Shaun, and although he was disappointed about losing her, he understood what she needed to do. She had trained a new eager and energetic girl to take over for her and felt confident that Shaun's business would continue to thrive.

On her last day at work, Jexi packed up the items from her desk. She heard the bell on the door jingle and looked up to see Brennan standing at the entrance. Her breath caught in her throat and she sat frozen as he walked toward her.

Surprisingly, she hadn't thought about him in weeks. She hadn't understood the freedom that God could bring until she surrendered those feelings to Him. She stood up and faced him.

"Hi, Jexi," Brennan said as he stopped at her desk.

"Hi, Brennan," she replied.

"How have you been?" Brennan asked.

"I've been really good, thanks," she answered. "What are you doing here? I didn't think you liked reading."

"I ran into your brother, and he told me that you worked here," Brennan explained. "So, I thought I'd come to see you. It looks like you're packing up your desk. Did you quit?"

"You didn't answer my question," Jexi said. "What are you doing here?"

"Yes, I did," Brennan snapped. "I came to see you."

"But why? What do you want?" Jexi asked.

"Just to see you," Brennan said.

"Okay, you've seen me. Have a good day," Jexi quipped.

Brennan looked surprised at her callous response. "I just wanted to talk to you. I miss you."

Jexi snorted. "You miss me?" she asked. "Does your girlfriend know you are here?"

Brennan looked surprised. "What . . . ? Um . . . how do you . . . ?" he stammered.

Jexi interjected. "I saw her. I went by your, no wait, our house and she was pulling into the driveway. She's pretty."

"Oh, you did?" Brennan asked as he hung his head. "I'm sorry. I never expected you to see her."

"I figured," replied Jexi. "But I guess that's how things go. So, you've seen me and you've talked to me. Anything else?"

Brennan cleared his throat and took a deep breath. "What's gotten into you? You've never been this harsh. You've always been so sweet. That's just one of the things I love about you. And I was . . . " he paused. "Well, I was actually hoping for another chance. I came to my senses, and I figured out that you are the one for me. I'm so sorry for how things went down. I broke things off with . . . her. I broke up with her for you," Brennan said.

Jexi laughed when she heard that. "You're not serious," she said. "You can't possibly be serious." Surprise filled Brennan's eyes. "Let me explain something to you. I am no longer the Jexi you knew. I've changed . . . and for the better. I've grown without you. I realized that you were darkness in my life that was holding me back. I have moved on, and I like my life the way it is. So, my answer is no."

Total confusion filled Brennan's face. "I don't understand. What do you mean? We are meant to be together; I see that now. Don't throw away what we have."

"Brennan, we are not meant to be together. We do not have anything anymore. YOU threw that away months ago. My life is on a completely different path now and it doesn't involve you," Jexi explained.

Brennan looked dejected and briefly, Jexi felt a little badly for him. But that feeling didn't last very long. She suddenly felt stronger and more confident than she had in all her life. She knew, at this moment, that God had cleared him from her mind and healed her pain. She was, without a doubt, over him. She didn't want him back. She didn't want to see his face. She didn't want to hear his voice.

Brennan attempted one more time to change her mind. "Please, Jex, don't turn me away. I already told you that I broke things off with the other girl. I did that because we are supposed to be together, and I knew you would take me back. We have to get back together. Please don't make me be alone."

Jexi looked at him with pity and spoke softly. "I am not the one making you be alone. You have done that to yourself. But I'll tell you what I'm going to do. I will pray for you. I will pray that you get what you want out of life and that you find true peace and happiness. Now, if you'll excuse me, my shift is over."

Brennan's face flashed with anger. "Really?" he sputtered. "After all our time together, this is how you treat me? You'll pray for me? You really are ridiculous, you know. I poured out my heart to you and you stomped on it. This makes you the bad guy here, not me!"

Jexi didn't flinch. She held up her hand as if to wave goodbye. "Bye, Brennan. I truly hope that you can find what you are looking for. I have to go clock out and you need to leave." With those words, she turned around and walked into the back room of the store.

Jexi's heart was pounding, and her hands were shaking as she let out a big breath. She had no idea that she would be able to stand up to Brennan like that. She knew that God alone had given her the strength she needed and that she knew that she was going to be okay. She quietly thanked God in her head for the help He had given her.

Shaun approached her and asked, "Are you okay, Jexi?"

Jexi smiled and responded, "Yes, I am more than okay. But will you make sure there is not a man standing by my desk before I come back out?"

Shaun peeked out of the back room and saw no one standing near Jexi's desk. He looked back at Jexi. "You mean the one you were talking to a minute ago?"

"Yeah, him. He's my ex-fiancée," said Jexi. "I don't want to go back out there unless he's gone."

Shaun looked out again and glanced around the store. He turned back to Jexi. "Looks like he's long gone," he said.

Jexi stepped out of the back room and walked to her desk. "Well, I guess I should go." She looked around the bookstore and looked at Shaun. This was harder than she expected it to be but if she lingered too long, it would be worse. She picked up the box that held her items. "I promise to keep in touch," she said as she walked toward the front.

Shaun waved as she walked away. "You'll always have a job here," he said just before she stepped out of the door and into her new life.

She couldn't wait to talk with Shaya that evening. She isn't going to believe how great I did! she thought to herself. She got into her car and sat down. She couldn't believe that she was still shaking. She picked up her phone and sent Shaya a quick text. You'll never guess what happened to me today! Then she drove home.

Jexi busied herself with packing when she got home. She opted to order Chinese food for dinner since most of the kitchen gadgets were packed and ready for the big move. After today, she was ready to get out of this place. She wondered if Brennan would look for her again. But honestly, she didn't care if he did or didn't. She really would pray for him. The ring of the doorbell interrupted her packing. She put down the tape and walked to the door to gather dinner.

Shaya arrived home at the same time that dinner was delivered. "Ooh, Chinese!" Shaya said. "Good choice!"

Jexi tipped the delivery driver and she and Shaya entered the apartment. They got some paper plates and napkins and sat down to eat. Shaya asked Jexi, "What happened at work today that was such big news?"

"You'll never guess who came to the bookstore," Jexi challenged.

"Someone famous?" guessed Shaya.

"Nope," said Jexi. "But I know you'll never get it in a million years, so I'll just tell you. So, get this. I'm packing up the last of my things from my desk right before my shift is over and Brennan walks through the door. Can you believe it?"

Shaya's mouth dropped open. She couldn't believe it and she prayed that Jexi hadn't fallen under that man's spell again. "You're kidding!" she said. "What did he say? Do I need to call your dad?"

"No, no need to call Dad," Jexi answered. "Brennan wanted me back."

Shaya groaned out loud. "Please tell me you didn't," she begged Jexi.

"I didn't!" Jexi said. "I told him that he is no longer a part of my life. He tried to say that I was being the bad guy and that I am the one throwing away what we had, but I didn't give in and I didn't cry! I told him that I would pray for him and that I hoped he would find happiness. And then, I walked away!"

Shaya put her hand in the air and said, "High five! I'm so proud of you. And, if I'm honest, very relieved."

"Thanks," Jexi said. "It was hard, but I could feel God giving me the strength to stand up to him. Brennan had the nerve to beg me to not make him be alone. I was able to tell him that he was the one doing that, not me!"

"So, you are completely over him?" Shaya asked. "Completely free of him? No more sadness over losing him?"

"Actually, no to the sadness part but yes, I am over him!" Jexi said. "I was surprised too! I think God showed me that I am truly free of him and that he is not a part of my future. I can be open to what comes next."

CHAPTER THIRTY

The line of vehicles arrived in Baxter Springs together. Shaya's car led the motorcade, followed by Jexi in her car, Ben in the moving van, and Attie in her car. Ben and Attie had driven to Kansas City the night before to help the girls with the big move. The four of them, along with Shaun, had loaded the van in just a few hours.

The entire crew was hungry and exhausted when they pulled into the back entrance to the diner. It was almost dinnertime, so Attie had called Aunt Katie ahead of time to have some dinner plates prepared for them. They would need to go inside to get the keys anyway, so they may as well stop to eat something before tackling the job of hauling things upstairs.

They all ate quickly because it would be getting dark soon and they did not want to be dragging things up the stairs in the dark.

Ben pushed his plate forward and stated, "I'm going to call Hunter to come and help us. No offense, but we are going to need some muscle to carry your furniture up those stairs."

Jexi gulped. She hadn't planned on seeing Hunter so soon. But she had to admit that Ben was right. She watched Ben walk off to contact Hunter and she said a silent prayer that she didn't look like a frightful mess. She excused herself to the restroom to check her reflection in the mirror. She wasn't pleased with what she saw. She quickly wrapped her hair in a messy ponytail and tried to smooth down any flyaway. She pinched her cheeks to redden them, like she had seen someone do on TV. Then she splashed a bit of water onto her face. She decided that it would have to suffice. Besides, her hairspray and comb were packed. She stopped for a moment and stared at herself in the mirror. Why am I making such a fuss? she wondered. I don't even like him that way! Or do I?

By the time she stepped out of the bathroom, the others had gone outside to survey the items to be moved. They had begun a discussion on what order things should be taken into the apartment. It was agreed by all that the bed and big furniture should go in before everything else. It was at this moment that Hunter arrived.

Hunter smiled and waved at the group. He flexed his muscles and asked, "Did someone call for these? The muscles are here. Let's lift some heavy things!"

Shaya rolled her eyes at Hunter's comment. "Okay, muscle man, get to work. The heavy stuff is in the truck."

Jexi couldn't help but laugh. Hunter noticed her giggle and walked to her to give her a quick hug. "Good to see you," he said. "Now, I gotta get to lifting!" He walked to the truck and he and Ben began carrying one of the bed frames out.

Jexi and Shaya went up the stairs together to unlock the door. The stairs at the back of the diner were fresh and new. There were ten steps up from the side that spilled onto a fairly large deck. "This is going to be a great place for some outdoor furniture and a grill," Jexi stated.

"And some flowers!" Shaya responded.

Jexi looked at her sideways. "Hello. Bees. Remember, I don't like bees and flowers bring the bees."

"Ugh!" Shaya said. "You're no fun."

"You can have some flowers inside the apartment," Jexi compromised.

Shaya smiled. "Okay, fair enough."

They continued up the remaining stairs until they reached the top. There was a small landing outside the door, just large enough for a small bench or pair of deck chairs. Shaya put the key in the lock and opened the door. They had only seen the place once and they really only noticed that Aunt Katie had good taste but hadn't really paid attention to the details. The door swung open to a bright and airy room. There were windows all around that allowed plenty of natural light. Perfect for indoor plants. Aunt Katie had created a beautiful open space that was large enough for a living area, a dining area, and a kitchen. There was an island designating a clear kitchen boundary. The kitchen sink was directly under one of the windows, which would be nice for watching the happenings on the street while washing dishes. Opposite of where they were standing was another door. This was the door that led into the diner below. To the right of where they stood was a door facing into the room and tucked into what seemed like a tiny hallway. "That must be the bathroom," Shaya pointed out. As the girls walked in that direction, they noticed the tiny hallway was where they found the two bedroom doors, directly across from one another. Both rooms were exactly the same, only opposite of one another. Both were small with closets in the corner and windows on the outside walls.

"It's smaller than our apartment in Kansas City but it's perfect for a fresh start. And the price is right!" Shaya told Jexi.

The girls continued to gush over the details of the apartment until they heard Ben's voice. "Heavy load coming through!" he announced. "Which room does this go in?" He and Hunter were carrying in one of the bed frames.

Shaya looked at Jexi. "We haven't decided on who gets which room!" she exclaimed.

"Really?" Hunter asked, sounding exasperated. "Hurry up, please. This thing isn't exactly light as a feather."

"They don't have any differences, so how about I take this one," Shaya said as she pointed to the room on the left.

"Sounds great!" Jexi responded.

"Um, yoo hoo," Ben interrupted. "Whose frame is this and which room does it go into?"

"Oh, sorry!" exclaimed Shaya. "That's mine. Put it in here." She pointed to her new bedroom.

The boys took the bed frame into the room on the left side of the hallway and set it down gently while breathing heavily.

"You are awfully winded for just a bed frame," Jexi teased. "Wait until you lug that big sofa up those stairs."

The next few hours were a flurry of activity. Attie had gone home since the stairs were challenging for her after the first couple of trips. She promised to come back tomorrow to help the girls unpack some of their boxes.

At nightfall, all of Jexi's and Shaya's belongings had been toted up to the apartment. Aunt Katie had brought some cold sodas and everyone sat down, completely drained.

"Ben," Shaya started. "Will you follow me in the moving van to drop it off tonight? If we don't get it there by this evening, they will charge an extra day."

Ben replied. "I'd rather not."

Shaya looked at him in stunned disappointment. "Really? You can't drop it off for me?"

"Of course, I can," Ben said. "But I can follow Hunter and he can give me a ride back. You girls have a lot to do before you can go to bed tonight. You take care of stuff here and we'll take care of the van for you." Ben looked at Hunter. "Is that okay with you, bud?"

"Sure!" Hunter exclaimed and stood up quickly. "Let's get to it!"

"Thank you so much," Shaya said to Ben and Hunter. "We really appreciate you both. This helps us out tremendously."

Jexi nodded. "Yes, thank you," she added. She turned towards Hunter. "Will I see you at church Sunday?"

Hunter smiled. "Absolutely! Where else would I be on a Sunday morning? There's nothing I like more than spending time in God's Word."

Jexi's stomach did a little flip. She grinned and blushed. I hope he doesn't notice that! she thought.

Ben approached Shaya to give her a kiss goodbye. "I'll call you when I get the van returned. Welcome home."

Shaya hugged him tight. "I'm happy to be back. I'll be waiting for your call," she said.

Hunter cleared his throat and said, "Ben, buddy, we should get going. It's getting late."

Aunt Katie yawned and stood up. "I'll be going too," she said. "The diner customers want breakfast early on Saturdays! You'll be glad to know I added extra layers of insulation to protect you from the noise up here. Good night!"

Shaya hugged her and said goodbye. After Aunt Katie had gone, Shaya sat down on the couch and looked around the living room filled with boxes. "I just need to find a blanket and a pillow. The rest can wait until tomorrow. Can you believe it? I'm not even going to brush my teeth."

Jexi laughed. "I won't tell anyone. We've had a long day and I get it. We can brush double in the morning. Any idea which box holds our bedding?"

Shaya walked from box to box reading the labels on each. "I'm so glad we labeled these!" she said. After a minute she said, "Aha! Found it!" She opened the box and pulled out pillows and blankets for both of them. She carried her bedding to her room. "We didn't think this through. Our beds are covered with boxes too. Why do we have so many boxes?" She went to work making a place to lie down.

Jexi went into her room and began moving boxes to the floor. When she finally cleared her bed, she tossed the blankets and pillows on the bed. "Mine is finally ready," she called to Shaya. "I'm sacking out! See you in the morning!" She laid down on her bed, covered herself up with a blanket, and shut her eyes.

"Goodnight," Shaya responded. She went back into the living room and switched off the lights. She sent Ben a text as she walked to her room. "Hey, I'm too tired to wait for your call. Would you mind if we just talk tomorrow?"

Ben replied right away. "Absolutely! Get your beauty rest. I love you."

Shaya smiled and drifted off to sleep immediately after she put down the phone.

CHAPTER THIRTY-ONE

Sunday morning, Jexi awoke with butterflies in her stomach. Hunter had not returned to help unpack Saturday, which was fine. She hadn't expected or asked him to help. The thought of seeing him this morning was nerve-racking, though. What was worse was that she could not figure out why she was responding to his presence in this way. She determined that when she saw him at church she would act completely cool and in control.

Attie, Shaya, and Jexi rode to church together. They walked in and went to the coffee shop to get some doughnuts and coffee. The coffee shop was one of the ways the church raised money to help fund mission work. As they placed their orders, Jexi read the acknowledgment plaque and couldn't help but be drawn into the pictures hanging in the little area. They were nothing like any place she had ever seen, except in Aunt Jessie's photos. She couldn't believe that other people had to live in such deplorable conditions. She made a mental note to talk to Aunt Jessie more about her mission work. She was very curious to know more.

They sat down to eat their breakfast and sip their coffee. Attie and Shaya talked with several people who greeted Attie and welcomed Shaya back to town. Shaya introduced Jexi to all of them and Jexi did her best to remember their names.

Ben walked over to their table and sat down with them. "I'm so happy that you're here!" he told Shaya. Shaya grabbed his hand and they continued to talk.

Jexi had tuned them out. She was very aware that she could be seeing Hunter at any moment, and she could barely keep her nerves settled.

As if on cue, she noticed Hunter across the coffee shop standing with a small group of other young adults. She debated within herself whether she should walk over to him to say hello. She couldn't ask Shaya, because Shaya was busy talking with Ben and her mother. She was a little surprised that he wasn't over here with Ben.

She had mustered the courage to talk with Hunter and was about to stand up when the group of people standing with Hunter shifted and Jexi could see why he wasn't over at their table talking with them. He was holding the hand of another girl. The girl was blond and beautiful. Jexi sucked in a breath so loud that everyone at the table looked at her. Shaya tapped her on the arm. "Are you okay?" Shaya asked.

"Hmm?" Jexi responded a bit flustered. She regained her composure quickly and stammered, "Oh, yeah, um, I'm fine."

"Then why did you just sound like you were gasping for air?" Shaya asked. "Did you forget to breathe?"

Jexi was quick on her feet and said, "I was just surprised at some of the pictures on the walls."

Shaya turned in the direction of Jexi's gaze and saw what had shocked her. Without another word to Jexi, she turned to Ben. "Hey, I see Hunter over there. Who is that girl he is with? You didn't tell me he was seeing someone."

Ben glanced over toward Hunter and said, "That is Amber. He started seeing her just after Thanksgiving."

Jexi felt like crying, but still could not understand why she was experiencing these feelings. She had no idea that she would feel the punch in the gut that she felt when she saw Hunter holding someone else's hand.

Shaya reached under the table and patted Jexi's knee in a silent and secret gesture of support. She wasn't surprised by Jexi's reaction. As much as her friend denied it, Shaya knew there were underlying feelings there for Hunter. Nobody else at the table seemed fazed by what had just happened. Shaya would not dare expose what she knew.

Jexi was relieved when Attie mentioned it was time to get into the worship center for service. She hoped that hearing a good message from God's Word would help her take her mind off Hunter. She wasn't there to see him anyway!

Just as they were about to walk in, Aunt Jessie came bursting through the door. "No time to talk," she announced, as she passed the group. "I need to get something to the tech guy and find Pastor Mike."

Shaya looked confused. "What was that all about? I didn't expect to see Aunt Jessie," she said.

"I think she is going to do a presentation about her mission work at the end of the service," responded Attie. "She is trying to recruit more missionaries."

"Oh, good!" exclaimed Jexi. "I have been hoping to hear more about her adventures."

Shaya looked at Jexi with surprise. "You have?" she asked.

Jexi smiled. "Yeah! She does such great and important work. It must feel nice to be a part of something so meaningful." She was relieved to have a distraction from Hunter.

They approached their seats as the band took the stage. Soon, Jexi found herself so lost in the worship songs that she forgot Hunter was the one leading them. She was able to close her eyes and put all of her focus on God. She had been reading in her Bible about praise and was learning how to express her praise through worship. She had read Psalm ninety-five, verses one and two, this morning before church. It read, "Come, let us sing for joy to the Lord; let us shout aloud to the Rock of our salvation. Let us come before Him with thanksgiving and extol Him with music and song." Jexi didn't know all the lyrics yet, but that didn't stop her from pouring her heart out to God in complete surrender.

Pastor Dave stepped up to the pulpit and welcomed everyone to the service. He surprised Shaya by announcing her arrival in town and letting everyone know that she would be taking over the position recently vacated at the church school. He asked her to stand as everyone clapped and cheered for her. She was embarrassed by the attention but, at the same time, she felt extremely proud to be stepping into a career that was completely God-centered. She knew in her heart that THIS is what God had always intended for her. She was thankful for His patience and grace while she spent so many years fumbling around doing the wrong thing.

Pastor Dave continued with prayer and his message for the day. "On this Christmas Eve, we celebrate the humble birth of our King, Jesus. Open your Bible to Luke two, seven." He paused to give everyone time to locate the verse and then began to read. "'Mary gave birth to Jesus and wrapped Him in swaddling cloth and laid Him in a manger.' We all know that Jesus was born to the virgin, Mary. We all know He was an unexpected King. We all know He was born in a stable and placed in a manger. Tonight, I would like us to look at another aspect of Jesus' birth.

"Many of us know that Jesus was wrapped in swaddling clothes and we often overlook this detail, but there is a great significance to these clothes. Swaddling clothes are strips of cloth, usually cotton, wrapped around a newborn. How could there be any importance in what Jesus was wrapped in?"

Pastor Dave paused and scanned the room. He took a deep breath and continued. "In the second chapter of Luke, we are told of an angel appearing to the shepherds tending their sheep. What many people don't know is that these shepherds weren't just ordinary shepherds. They were Levitical shepherds, raising sacrificial lambs for Passover. These lambs had to be perfect and flawless, so when a sacrificial lamb was born, it was wrapped in swaddling clothes and kept away from the other sheep. This is why the angel told the shepherds what the baby would be wearing. Listen to Luke two, verse ten, 'And the angel said to them: Fear not; for, behold, I bring you good tidings of great joy, that shall be to all the people: For, this day, is born to you a

Savior, who is Christ the Lord, in the city of David. And this shall be a sign unto you. You shall find the infant wrapped in swaddling clothes and laid in a manger.'

"The shepherds would know what swaddling clothes were because of their work with the sacrificial sheep, so they would easily recognize the material that wrapped Jesus. Therein lies the importance of the clothes. In addition, being swaddled in this manner foreshadowed Jesus as being the flawless Lamb of God who would bring salvation to the world by being sacrificed.

Jexi looked over at Shaya, who was feverishly writing notes. She leaned over to her and whispered, "I had never heard that before."

Shaya smiled and whispered back, "Neither had I, but that's pretty cool."

Pastor Dave continued to talk about the birth of Jesus and Jexi couldn't help but feel overwhelming sadness that Baby Jesus was born, just to be sacrificed for humankind. What a heavy burden for Him to carry throughout His life. She wondered when He found out His role in God's plan. She made a mental note to ask Shaya about that later.

Toward the end of the sermon, the congregation took communion. Jexi was filled with emotions as she took part in her first communion. She realized that in taking the bread and the juice, she was honoring one of Jesus' promises to the world. Pastor Dave read Mark fourteen, twenty-two through twenty-five. "While they were eating, Jesus took bread, and when He had given thanks, He broke it and gave it to His disciples, saying, 'Take it; this is My body. Then He took a cup, and when He had given thanks, He gave it to them, and they all drank from it. This is My blood of the covenant, which is poured out for many,' He said to them. 'Truly I tell you, I will not drink again from the fruit of the vine until that day when I drink it new in the kingdom of God.'"

Jexi marveled at the comparison between the bread and juice to Jesus' body and blood. She was consumed with gratitude that Jesus had sacrificed Himself for her. She felt a tear escape and roll down her cheek. It hit her suddenly that this love is what she had been longing for her entire life.

CHAPTER THIRTY-TWO

When the communion song ended, Aunt Jessie took the stage and introduced herself. The congregation giggled a little and Aunt Jessie quipped, "Okay, so everyone already knows me."

She asked the man in the sound booth to open the slide show she had given him before church and then proceeded. "I have something very important to share. As many of you know, I am a missionary liaison to people in Honduras. I have just received word that the small school there is in desperate need of books and supplies. The people of the village are in need of shoes and toys for the children. I am preparing to visit them in March, but I am requesting your help. Not only are we asking for people to donate items, but I am seeking volunteers to go with me to take the supplies down.

"We are not able to just ship things to the village because the boxes get stolen somewhere in transport. The people have been unable to figure out why this is happening, but in the meantime, we will continue to deliver them in person by taking them on the flights when we go. I have a list of items needed that will be available in the lobby after the service. Also, if you would like to volunteer to package the items for shipment or volunteer to help deliver the packages, there is a sign-up sheet as well. Please indulge me for a moment, as I introduce some of the villagers I have met."

The slideshow started and Jessie took time with each photo to explain the subject they were viewing. "This is Juan Carlos, his wife Angelica, and their six children." The congregation shared exaggerated mumbles about the six children and Jessie continued. "The oldest son is Juan Carlos, Jr., but we call him JC. JC and his sister Carlita were born to Juan Carlos' first wife, Isabella. She died giving birth to Carlita." Again there were murmurs amongst the crowd about how sad it was that Isabella passed away. Jessie moved on, "Angelica was just nineteen when she married Senior." Jessie smiled at the memory of this family. "Juan Carlos and Angelica are doting parents. Diego is the first son of Angelica and Juan Carlos. He is fourteen. Dante is twelve, Sophia is nine, and Natalia is four. I won't lie. I have grown to love this family very much. They are solid in Christ and hold their own church in the same building used for their school in the village."

She clicked on the next slide. "This is Carlos and Anita. They are the aging parents of Juan Carlos, Sr., and not in the best of health. The entire village works together to help one another but Juan Carlos and Angelica are pretty much the unspoken leaders. They take care of Senior's parents and their children, but they also pitch in to make sure the village is well managed. Juan Carlos also serves as the village's pastor.

"The village is mostly self-sufficient. They grow their own crops and raise many of the animals they need for food. There is a stream nearby where they are able to get clean water." Jessie clicked through several photos of the village, the land, the stream, and various families. She stopped at a photo with twelve young children, all smiling at the camera. The children were writing with extremely small pencils on old, yellowed paper. "These are the children of the village at school. You will recognize that it is the same building where they meet for church. There aren't many buildings, and they don't have much so they don't mind using the same space," Jessie explained.

Jexi's heart hurt for those children. She made a plan to go shopping for supplies as soon as she could. In the midst of her thoughts, she sucked in a breath. Wait, she thought, I can contact Shaun to see if he would be willing to donate some books. He often gets used books that would work just as well. She couldn't wait to call him!

Walking to the lobby after the service, Jexi was extremely excited about her ability to help these villagers. She searched for Aunt Jessie so that she could share her ideas. While she looked around to spot her, her eyes fell on Hunter. Standing next to him was Amber. She was holding his arm and talking with friends. Hunter caught Jexi's gaze and for a brief second Jexi froze. She didn't want him to think that she was looking at him, so she quickly glanced away and set about looking for Jessie again. To her relief, Jexi found her within moments, and she headed straight for her.

Jessie was talking with another couple in the church when Jexi approached her. Jexi waited so as to not interrupt their conversation. When they were finished, Jexi blurted out her ideas all in one breath. "Aunt Jessie, I want to help the people in Honduras! I am going to go shopping as soon as I can for supplies. But I also have an old boss in Kansas City who owns a bookstore! I am going to contact him to see if he will donate books to us! I know he will help!"

Jessie laughed, "Slow down, Jexi! I am thrilled that you are so excited. I love the idea of contacting your old boss. If he can help, that would be fantastic. But, let me run something by you. How about you come with me to deliver the supplies in March? We can use all the hands that we can get, and you seem to be so excited about helping the people in Honduras."

Jexi's exuberance waned quickly. She took in a slow breath. "Um, go with you?" she asked.

"Sure!" replied Jessie. "You will be forever changed. I can't tell you how being involved with missions has drawn me closer to God!"

Jexi stuttered, "I already promised Aunt Katie that I'd help in the diner. And I am so new at this God stuff. And doesn't that cost money? And I don't want to risk getting kidnapped."

Jessie scoffed. "Oh, girl, you are too funny!" she quipped. "Let's make time for you and me to talk. In the meantime, just think about it, okay? Come by my house one evening this week." Another group of people walked up that caught Jessie's attention.

Jexi nodded her head but didn't say anything. She was grateful for the distraction and walked away with a heavy heart. She really did want to help these people, but actually going to a different country was a terrifying prospect. She just moved to Baxter Springs. She couldn't leave Shaya like that. It was clearly a bad idea.

That evening, the girls gathered at Attie's house for dinner. Shaya loved being home and close to her mom. She had missed her mom and these moments while living in Kansas City. She didn't regret moving up there because it had been a growing experience for her, and she had met Jexi. But being back home felt right. She was very thankful Jexi had agreed to come with her. She walked over to Jexi and gave her an impromptu hug.

Jexi looked stunned. "What the heck? What's wrong? Are you sick or something?"

Shaya laughed. "No, I just wanted to give you a hug. Just say thanks and let it go."

Jexi looked at her and giggled. "You just made it weird."

All of the ladies burst out into laughter and even Jexi felt that warm at-home feeling. She was glad she had come with Shaya. She was thankful that Shaya's family embraced her as one of their own. She thought about Jessie's suggestion from this morning. How could she leave this circle of love that surrounded her?

Attie jumped up and quickly placed a bag of popcorn in the microwave. She then moved to the living room and turned on the television. "Movie time!" she hollered.

Shaya grabbed Jexi by the hand. "It's time for our Christmas Eve tradition! We watch It's a Wonderful Life. I love this movie! We've watched it every Christmas Eve since I was little!"

"I've never seen it," commented Jexi.

Attie and Shaya both whipped around and stared at Jexi with mouths wide open. At that very moment, the microwave dinged. Jexi felt a little awkward with their stares, so she yelped, "I'll grab the popcorn!"

Shaya laughed at her friend. "Don't take too long!" she called after Jexi. "We will start without you if we have to!"

Jexi returned a moment later with three bowls of popcorn and they all sat down and waited for Attie to start the movie. Attie pressed play on the remote and the television sprang to life with the black-and-white movie.

They had just watched the scene where George was wishing he had never been born. Shaya's phone rang and she subtly viewed the display. "Oh, my gosh! It's my dad!" She jumped up and ran up the stairs as she accepted the call, "Hello?"

Jexi turned to Attie, "I didn't think her dad was involved in her life," she said quizzically.

Attie pressed pause on the movie. "He hasn't been," she answered. "I don't have any contact with him either and as far as I know, neither of us even know where he is. I'm surprised he's calling her." Jexi noticed that she seemed a bit uncomfortable.

"I'm sure it will be fine," she tried to assure Attie.

"Yeah, maybe," Attie muttered. It was clear that she was concerned for her daughter. "I needed a stretch break anyway. I'm all stove-up." Attie walked to the kitchen to put away dinner dishes.

Jexi sat alone in the living room. She wondered what it would be like to not know her father. She was always so blessed with both of her parents and her heart went out to them both.

Attie and Shaya both returned to the living room and Shaya immediately picked up the remote and hit play. "Back to the show! Thanks for pausing," she announced.

Jexi looked at her with shock. "You aren't going to tell us what happened?" she asked.

Shaya put her finger to her lips and shook her head. "Shhh," she said, "the movie is back on."

Jexi shrugged and turned her attention back to the movie. She knew that after Shaya had some time to process, she'd be more willing to open up. Throughout their friendship, she had learned to give Shaya space and time. Evidently, this event required both.

When Attie shut the movie off, Shaya looked at Jexi and asked, "What did you think?"

"That was really great!" Jexi answered. "I'm so glad that George decided that life really was good after all. That part where no one recognized him was hard to watch. But my favorite scene was the one where ZuZu said, 'Every time a bell rings, an angel gets his wings.' That was so sweet." She turned to Shaya. "Now spill."

"Oh, alright," Shaya agreed. "Dad called."

"You are so exasperating!" Jexi groaned.

Shaya giggled. "Oh, no! She's using the big words on me. I'm in trouble."

Attie giggled and interjected. "I would like to know what happened also, dear. Are you okay?"

"I think I am," Shaya answered. "I'll admit I was surprised to hear from him. But all he wanted was to say Merry Christmas and that he missed me. He mentioned he wants to see me and talk."

"Are you going to meet with him?" asked Jexi.

"Nah, not right now," Shaya said. "He's kept me waiting all these years, he can wait a little while longer."

Attie looked stunned. "Is he here? Is he in town?" she asked.

"No," Shaya replied, "he's in Montana somewhere. But he said he could fly me out there or he is open to making a trip here soon. I told him that he didn't need to rush."

Attie tried to help soften the situation. "I know you're angry, sweetheart, but you need to try to let the resentment go."

Shaya's calm demeanor melted, and she stiffened a bit. "Easy for you to say, Mom. But where has he been all these years? Why has he acted like I don't exist? And what right does he have to act like that? Don't I have a right to be at least a little bit angry?"

Attie stood up and walked to her desk to get her Bible. She sat back down and began searching the Scriptures. She stopped on a page.

"Here it is. Matthew eighteen, twenty-one, and twenty-two. 'Then Peter came to Him and asked, "Lord, how often should I forgive someone who sins against me? Seven times?" "No, not seven times," Jesus replied, "but seventy times seven."'"

Shay started to interject. "But . . . ."

Attie held up her hand in front of her daughter's face. "I'm not finished." She turned a few more pages. "Ephesians four, thirty-one and thirty-two. 'Let all bitterness and wrath and anger and clamor and slander be put away from you, along with all malice. Be kind to one another, tenderhearted, forgiving one another, as God in Christ forgave you.'"

"Okay, okay," Shaya started.

"Pipe down and listen," Attie interrupted. "Luke seventeen verse four. 'Even if that person wrongs you seven times a day and each time turns again and asks forgiveness, you must forgive.' Shall I go on?"

Shaya looked at the floor. "No, I get what you're saying. I can't make any promises, but I'll work on it."

Jexi, who had been silent throughout their conversation, spoke out. "I forgave Brennan, remember? You can do this too! I don't know your history with your dad, Shay, but he's your dad. I think you should forgive him. It sounds like he wants the chance to make things right."

"And one more thing," Attie added, "Jesus commands us to forgive. Even He was able to forgive the people who put Him on that cross."

Shaya softened. "Yes, I know. He asked God to forgive them for they knew not what they were doing," she admitted. "But for me, it's going to take some time. I'm not as good as Jesus."

"That's fair," Jexi said, giggling which caused Attie to laugh.

Shaya couldn't resist and began chuckling also. "I'm ready to go home and get into bed. Plus, I told Ben I'd call him."

Attie reached for her daughter's hand and invited Jexi to grab her other hand. "Let me pray for you before you leave." They all bowed their heads together as Attie spoke. "Gracious and Heavenly Father, thank You for readily offering Your forgiveness to us and for pouring out Your love. I ask that You show Shaya how to forgive her earthly father and fill her with Your strength as she navigates this renewed relationship. Cover her with Your protection to keep her heart from being broken again. Father, thank You for giving her a second chance to know her dad. In Jesus' name, Amen."

Shaya looked up at Attie and smiled. "Thanks, Mom," she said as she hugged her.

CHAPTER THIRTY-THREE

Christmas Day and the week following had been busy. Jexi had gone shopping for school supplies and contacted Shaun about donating books to Honduras. She had met with Aunt Jessie to talk about the mission trip and was still not convinced that she should go. Part of her thought it would be a fun adventure, but she didn't think she was quite brave enough.

When she mentioned the trip to Shaya, she told Jexi that it would be a once-in-a-lifetime opportunity and that she should go. But even that encouragement hadn't solidified a decision for her. She continued to pray about what she should do.

Jexi hadn't seen Hunter since Christmas Eve and if she was honest with herself, she had been a little hurt by seeing him with someone else. She felt as if he really liked her but maybe not as much as she thought. And perhaps he wasn't the one God had in mind for her. Life could be so confusing.

Shaya was dressing and primping for her New Year's Eve date with Ben. "I'm a little nervous. Ben said he had a special evening planned but won't give me any hints. He just said to dress in something warm."

"It is going to be fabulous, as always," Jexi said. "Ben could probably dress you in a potato sack and take you to the hot dog joint and you'd be happy. It's cute that you still get nervous."

Shaya smiled. "He still gives me butterflies, even after all these years!" she said. "I love that about him! What are your plans for tonight? You aren't staying here alone, are you?"

"Oh, not much," Jexi answered. "I'm going to your mom's to play cards with Aunt Jessie and Aunt Katie. They want to try to teach me how to play a new game. They seem excited to have a fourth player."

"Be careful," Shaya warned. "Remember, Mom cheats."

"Oh, and your mom said to wear my pajamas. I guess it's going to be a sleepover, so don't worry if I don't come home tonight. I'm concerned that the old gals won't make it to midnight." Jexi commented as she exploded with laughter.

"I'm glad that you'll be in safe hands," commented Shaya. She looked at her watch. "Oh, Ben will be here any minute! How do I look? Is my hair okay? Should I have worn less makeup? I can wipe some off." She reached into the closet and pulled out two coats. "Which one should I wear?"

Jexi smiled and pointed to the coat on the left. "That one," she answered. "You look perfect. Ben will be blown away."

The doorbell chimed and Jexi ran to open the door for Ben. He smiled broadly when he saw Shaya. "You are beautiful," he gushed.

"Thanks," Shaya said.

Jexi giggled. "I'll leave you two to your evening. Have fun! I need to get into my jammies." She walked back into her bedroom.

"Where are we going?" Shaya asked. "You haven't told me anything!"

"You'll find out as you need to," Ben answered. "First, we need to stop in at the diner."

"But the diner is closed for the night," Shaya objected.

"I know, just trust me," Ben replied.

The two walked to the front entrance of the diner and Shaya saw why they were stopping by the diner. All the tables except for one had been moved to the sides of the restaurant. The last table sat alone in the middle of the room with candles lit and the most beautiful china plates Shaya had ever seen. There were two chairs on either side of the table and candles placed on the floor surrounding the table in a heart shape. A bouquet of flowers was also on the table and soft romantic music was being piped through the speakers. There were fairy lights hanging from the ceiling, illuminating the room in a soft glow. Shaya was pleasantly surprised at how romantic everything looked and she gasped when she saw Aunt Katie standing at the door of the kitchen.

"I thought you were at Mom's playing cards," Shaya asked Katie.

"Well, I can't help to pull off a surprise if I tell you absolutely everything, now, can I?" Katie chuckled. "You two go ahead and sit down. Dinner will be served shortly." She ducked back into the kitchen.

Ben and Shaya sat down and immediately Katie emerged carrying a meal platter. She sat the platter down on the table and lifted the cover. The aroma of the meal almost made Shaya drool. She and Ben laughed and talked throughout dinner while Katie made sure they had all they needed. When dinner was over, Ben offered to help Katie clean up the mess.

"Don't be ridiculous," Katie said. "You two get on with your evening. I'll take care of everything." She winked at Ben as she turned and carried the first load of dishes to the kitchen.

"Thanks, Aunt Katie," Ben said. "I couldn't have done this without your help."

"Now where?" asked Shaya.

"What do you mean? What makes you think there's another location? Maybe that's all you get," Ben said as he smiled at Shaya.

Shaya pretended to pout. "It's still early on New Year's Eve," she said. "Our date isn't going to be over that quickly, is it?"

Ben laughed and pulled her close to him. "No, it isn't," he whispered into her ear. "Just trust me."

They walked out and got into his car, and he began to drive. As they passed through the curvy roads Shaya finally asked, "Are we going to Joplin?"

"Yep," he replied.

"Where in Joplin?" Shaya asked.

"TRUST ME!" Ben exclaimed with feigned frustration.

Shaya giggled. "Okay, I'll stop asking."

They rode in silence for the remainder of the drive. When they stopped, Shaya noticed that they were at the waterfalls of Joplin.

"I remember this place!" she exclaimed. "It is so pretty! But It looks like someone is here." Shaya pointed to a spot on the rocks that was lit up with lanterns.

Ben reached for her hand. "No, that's for us," he explained.

Shaya gasped. "Really?"

"Yes, really," Ben answered.

They approached the lit-up area and Shaya could see a blanket on the ground near the falls. She saw four battery-powered lanterns, one on each corner of the blanket. They sat down and allowed their feet to dangle over the edge of the hanging rock. Ben reached into a nearby basket, pulled out another blanket, and laid it across their laps.

"How did you know I'd be cold?" Shaya asked, laughing.

"Because you're always cold," Ben replied. "I made sure I was prepared."

Shaya rested her head on Ben's shoulder. "We had our first kiss here, remember?"

"Of course, I remember," Ben answered. "I've never forgotten. No matter what has happened between us over the years, I haven't forgotten anything. I also remember how I felt after that first kiss."

Even in the darkness, Shaya could see the beauty that surrounded them. She smiled. "I never forgot either. You have always been the love of my life," she said.

Without Shaya knowing it, Ben glanced over his shoulder and nodded. Then he gently guided Shaya to stand up. "Are we leaving already?" Shaya asked.

"No, I'd like to have this dance," Ben said. He pressed play on his phone and their favorite song echoed out.

Shaya laughed. "You have always been so silly," she mentioned. She took his arms and began to sway with him to the music. After a minute, Ben stopped dancing and took one step back.

"What's wrong?" Shaya asked.

"Nothing," Ben replied. "Absolutely nothing. As a matter of fact, things couldn't be more perfect." He lowered himself to one knee and reached into his pocket.

Shaya gasped. "What's going on?" she asked.

Ben started talking. "Shaya, you have always been the one. I have known that from the moment we had our first kiss right here. God has blessed me with a second chance, and I don't intend to waste it. I know for a fact that I want no one else but you to be by my side for the rest of my life. You are more special to me than you'll ever know, and I never want to lose you again. I love you with my whole heart. Will you please do me the honor of being my wife?"

By the end of Ben's proposal, Shaya was crying her best ugly cry. She squealed loud enough to wake up everyone in the neighborhood. "YES! A million times, YES!" She grabbed his shirt and yanked him up from the ground. She threw herself into his arms and gave him a long, hard kiss.

Shaya was startled by a loud whoop from beyond the trees and a person stepped toward them. Shaya jumped behind Ben and screeched, "Who is that?!"

Ben put his hand on her arm, "It's just Ron, don't worry."

"Why in the world is your brother here?" Shaya asked.

"I wanted him to get our engagement on video," Ben explained. "That's all."

"Oh, my stars!" Shaya exclaimed. "We are engaged! There is so much to do! I can't wait to tell my mom and start shopping for my dress! I wonder if Aunt Katie will cater for us." She suddenly remembered that she had been crying and must look like a frightful mess. "And here I am, ugly crying and everything, on video!"

"Shay, you are as beautiful as always," Ben said.

Shaya kissed him again. "Thanks," she said. "Now let's go tell the world! Good to see you, Ron."

Ben caught Shaya's arm as she started toward the car. "It's so late, Shaya, we can just tell everyone tomorrow."

"There's no way I can keep this to myself until tomorrow!" Shaya said with giddiness. "Please, please, please take me to my mom's," she begged.

He turned toward his brother and asked, "Do you mind taking the blankets and lanterns with you? I guess we are leaving right now."

Ron happily agreed to pick up the items on the rocks and bid the happy couple goodbye.

At Attie's house, no one was able to stay awake until midnight. Attie was in her bedroom, her sisters were in the guest room, and Jexi was sacked out on the couch in the living room. Jexi was jolted awake by the sound of Shaya bursting through the front door.

"Where is everyone?" Shaya hollered.

Jexi rubbed her eyes. "We're all sleeping," she answered.

"Well, we need to get everyone up right now!" said Shaya.

Jexi glanced at Ben who looked a bit embarrassed. "What is wrong?" she asked in a panic.

Shaya began walking toward her mother's room, "No, nothing is wrong, we just need to talk to you all!" She banged on her mother's bedroom door. "Mama! Get up!"

Aunt Katie and Aunt Jessie stepped out of the guest room with sleepy eyes. "Child, what is the matter with you?" Aunt Jessie asked. "Don't you remember your manners? By thunder, what's all the racket about?"

Attie then stepped out of her bedroom and glared at Shaya. "You had better be severely hurt," she growled.

"Even better, Mama!" Shaya shrieked. "Come out into the living room, everyone!"

Everyone grumbly followed her into the living room where Jexi was waiting. Aunt Katie spoke first. "This had better be good. I can't stand being woken up like that!"

Shaya laughed and put her left hand up into the air, waving it around. Still quite sleepy, no one understood what she was doing. Attie waved back at her. "Hello," Attie said, as realization struck and she noticed a shimmer coming off of Shaya's hand. "That's . . . is that what I think it is . . . ?" she trailed off.

"WE ARE ENGAGED!" Shaya yelled happily.

All of a sudden, the mood in the room lightened as everyone smiled and jumped up to hug and congratulate the young couple. Shaya was busy showing off the ring and telling the story of how Ben proposed. Attie was crying with happiness.

Jexi stepped back and watched the jubilee. She was so happy for her best friend. She always knew that Ben and Shaya would get married someday and she also knew how ecstatic it made Shaya to be with Ben. But it hit her that Shaya would be moving in with Ben after they were married. What does that mean for me? she thought. I can't afford to live anywhere else. And certainly, Aunt Katie won't let me stay in that apartment after Shaya gets married. She felt selfish thinking that way, but it was a valid concern. The thought of Honduras flashed in her mind again followed by a quick vision of Hunter with Amber. Jexi closed her eyes and said a silent prayer. "Lord, guide me down the right path. Show me what to do. Not my will, but Yours. In Jesus' name, Amen." She opened her eyes and saw Aunt Jessie standing next to her.

"Aunt Jessie," she started.

"Yes, honey," Jessie answered.

Jexi inhaled deeply and let it out slowly. She knew what to do. "I'm going with you to Honduras," she said quietly.

www.ingramcontent.com/pod-product-compliance
Lightning Source LLC
Chambersburg PA
CBHW032109090426
42743CB00007B/296